SOME LIKE IT ROYAL

GOING ROYAL
BOOK ONE

HEATHER LONG

ISBN: 978-1-956264-94-4

For Nan, because she read me my very first romance and taught me to never, ever give up on my dreams. If I wanted something, I had to be willing to fight for it.

FOREWORD

Dear Reader,

Thank you for picking up *Some Like it Royal*. For those of you who've read me for a while, you might be thinking this title is familiar. You wouldn't be wrong, The very first draft of this book dates to 2011. Eventually, in late 2012 it was contracted by Carina Press, a digital imprint of Harlequin. It released in January of 2014.

It literally released a week or so after I'd had the first of three spinal surgeries I would have over the next decade. I was in a tremendous amount of pain, but the release week was filled with games and parties and so much fun in my group that it kept a smile on my face.

Alyx and Daniel were very much my rom com couple. I loved their interactions, their first kiss (and seriously their first kiss remains my favorite of all that I've ever written) and their love story. It's different from what my current readers may be used to, particularly as it's done in third person.

Let me tell you, that took me a hot minute to reacclimatize too when I was editing. I also added scenes, rearranged some, and gave the spicy scenes a little more zest. I also needed to bring the story up to date a little more. It's a little weird to realize just how much the world has changed in the decade and change since this was first written.

Still, I am so excited to share this with you and I hope you enjoy this little throwback to a different style of storytelling. You'll notice this one is dedicated to my nan. She was the one who introduced me to Harlequins and gave me such a love for them.

So this book really is for her and for those of us who love the "fairy tale shit" that often underscores so much romance.

Happy reading!

xoxo

Heather

CHAPTER I
ALYX

The pounding on the side of the car jerked her awake. Alyx shoved up her sleep mask and glared blearily at the window of her Volvo. If the cops seriously planned to make her move again, she might lodge a complaint with the city. The parking garage was *open to the public* and she didn't pull in until after it opened. She'd parked in the back corner of the roof, on purpose, to avoid taking any choice parking from day dwellers.

But the blond haired, blue-eyed god cupping his hands against the glass to see past the glare did not look like a cop. Grumbling, she unfolded herself from the blanket. She'd just found the perfect position for her legs and back—one that wouldn't leave her cramped awkwardly when it was time to get up.

She waved a hand at him as if to say "what?" and he answered with a two-knuckled knock on the glass and rolling his finger as though miming the window opening. She sighed. Yeah, he might appear lickable, but she was about to get a ticket and she hadn't paid for the last one yet.

Shoving the blanket off, she reached over and shoved the key in so she could roll down the window—but only partially. "Look, Officer, I'm sorry. I was too tired to drive home, and I thought I'd park here safely and get some Z's."

"Really? That's why you pulled in two hours ago and hunkered down? And you've parked here for the last three mornings to sleep?" Hot caramel poured over ice cream didn't sound as good as his voice. The pure liquid sex in the deep baritone ripped the cobwebs of sleep out of her mind and she crawled forward to peer up at him.

She knew him.

It was *that* guy from the restaurant—great tipper and really cute, but he'd seemed eager. Too eager.

Crap.

"You're not a cop." Grumpy accusation hung in the air. It was one thing for a cop to rouse her from sleep, but another for the guy who'd sat in her station night after night, staring at her with wild speculation in his eyes. Years of bouncing from foster home to foster home gave her radar for people who wanted something from her. She didn't know what his game was, but...*ugh. No, thank you.* Determined to ignore him, she pressed the button to raise the window once more.

"Wait." He thrust his hand through to catch the glass and I took the pressure off the button before I crushed those fingers. He held up a carrier with two oversized cups of coffee from

Dancing Goats. It was one of her favorite coffee shops, both for the coffee they made and the ambience. Also, they didn't charge extra for using milk alternatives like oat milk. The scent hit her with a vicious allure. Okay, she might forgive him for waking her up. Maybe. "Can we talk?"

He wanted something. Why else bring her coffee? Of course he wanted something.

She sighed.

"Ten minutes. All I'm asking for is ten minutes. I brought coffee. There're croissants too." He let go of the window to grab the paper bag off the tray and dangled it invitingly.

Bastard. But her stomach growled at the thought. She'd skipped her free meal the night before—the dinner shift had been slammed and she needed the extra tips to cover the weekend immersion class coming up in Santa Monica. Cutting another look at him, she weighed her options. If she ignored him, he'd probably knock again or report her. Either way, it wasn't worth the hassle.

"Fine. Ten minutes. Back away from the door," she ordered and waited until he complied before disentangling the last of the blanket. After tugging the key out, she scooted over to climb out of the passenger side of the car. It was away from him. That let her straighten her shorts and tank top to something a little more presentable.

Finger combing her tousle of red hair, she wished she'd tucked the ponytail holder around her wrist. It was what she usually did, but last night's shift left her dead on her feet by two a.m.

and she'd still had to drive five miles to the parking garage.

Maybe she should really think about getting an apartment. But the ones she could afford were dumps or so far out, it would cost her even more to drive back and forth. Worse, if she sank all of her money into a place to live, she wouldn't be able to take classes.

A lose-lose proposition all the way around.

She squinted across the top of the car. Mr. Godlike kept his distance, but damn if the man didn't look fantastic. Bronze skin, white button-down shirt open at the collar and sleeves rolled up. His dress slacks weren't wrinkled and his blond hair curled just slightly toward his face. He didn't even have the grace to look a bit stubbly and rumpled.

Padding barefoot around the car, she held out her hand for the coffee. He handed it to her and opened his mouth, but silenced when she held up a finger. She inhaled the sweet fragrance of the coffee and considered taking a sip—just one, what could it hurt? But the guy was a few slices shy of a full loaf and this was LA. With great regret, she set the cup on top of her car.

Beware strangers bearing gifts...

"You have ten minutes. Go." She leaned back against her car, cradling her Taser in her hand. He frowned and looked at the bag of croissants and then over at her again. She shook her head. If she wasn't drinking his coffee, she wouldn't take his tasty pastries either—no matter how good they smelled.

Sighing, he took his own coffee cup out before setting the holder on the black Lexus she hadn't noticed parked right next to hers. With exaggerated care, he took a long drink before leaning back against his vehicle, mirroring her pose.

"My name is Daniel Voldakov. I own Spherecast Technologies." He paused as if she should recognize the name.

Lifting her eyebrows, she glanced meaningfully at her watchless wrist.

"We're the fastest-growing software company in the States. I've made great strides in Canada and South America, but we can't get traction in the European Union markets. Too many competitors from old families there." Irritation discolored the words. "But I have an opportunity that I'd like to explore and a proposal for you..."

Alyx sighed, rolling her head from side to side to relieve the crackle of tension stiffening the muscles. She concentrated on keeping her expression bland, waiting. The scent of the dark-roast coffee kept tormenting her, but her grip on the Taser remained firm.

"If you'll agree to marry me—and by that, I mean you don't have to actually marry me, but we *will* have to be engaged—and lend me the use of your royal title, I can make the acquaintance of the Andraste Grand Duke, Armand. Once we've cemented that introduction, I could use his influence to open the EU markets for the company."

The man spoke English. The words and the accent were exceptionally clear. But the so-called proposal rang madness in her ears. "I'm sorry, what?"

"Marry me. Be engaged to me. I'll take care of your bills, get you a real place to sleep and all you have to do is be my princess and help me get those invitations." He swallowed another mouthful of coffee and took a step forward. "Look, I know it will take a lot of work on both our parts. But we can definitely do this. You'll be amply compensated. I promise."

Yeah, she really should have just opened the door and used the Taser on him. While he twitched into unconsciousness, she could have driven away. Better, she shouldn't have opened the car door at all, just started the car and gotten the hell out of here.

As casually as she could manage, she scanned the upper lot of the downtown Los Angeles parking garage. Unfortunately, at six-thirty in the morning, no one else seemed to need to park up here.

They were alone.

"I've got a great place in Beverly Hills. Twenty rooms, six bedrooms—you can have your pick. I'll throw in all the clothes you'll need and any-thing designer we pick up for events. They would be yours to keep." He held out the verbal entice-ment like she was some kind of stray dog who would leap at the offer of a free meal.

Not that she wasn't wishing she could drink his coffee and dive into the bag with the crois-sants in it, but that was hardly the point. "Do I look like a prostitute to you?"

Probably not the best question considering she stood there barefoot in shorts and a thin yellow tank top, but still...

"I'm not offering you money for sex, Princess. I understand who you are. I'm just offering you an opportunity to be *someone* and help me out at the same time. It's a win-win proposition." Strangely, his tone echoed with sincerity, but the words flirted with insanity.

"You think just because I'm an actress looking for work, I'm going to agree to some farce of a marriage so you can get me alone? So maybe I look stupid to you." He could be Ted Bundy—or worse, Jeffrey Dahmer. All the serial killers in the movies looked sweet and some looked sexy. He didn't smell like a meth head, but that didn't mean he wasn't whacked out on something.

Pity, too. Because anyone who looked as good as he did should really not be a drug addict.

"No, Princess." He took a step forward and she raised the Taser, looking to keep her options open if she had to run. She could shock him and leave him drooling on the concrete. Not a lot he could do with a twelve hundred volts running through his system.

He stopped and held up his free hand, open and palm forward. "Maybe I should start over."

"Maybe you should get back in your car and go back to whatever wonderland you escaped from and we'll forget all about this." It was too far to run for the stairs, but she might make it around the car and back inside.

"Princess, I understand that you may not

want to advertise your heritage, particularly if you're living out of a car. But I'm the guy who can put you on top. That's got to be worth something."

Yeah, a one-way ticket to a hugging jacket was what it was worth.

"What's with the princess shtick? Do you think if you say it enough it will happen? Like Beetlejuice?" She suddenly didn't want the coffee anymore.

The man—*Daniel Voldakov, remember his name, you may need to report him to the cops*—sighed and pinched the bridge of his nose. "Princess, let me start at the beginning?"

"I'm thinking your ten minutes are up. I listened. I'm not interested. Thanks for the coffee." She jogged right and made it to the trunk of her car and around to the other side. He remained next to his vehicle—thankfully—a look of consternation wrinkling his forehead.

"Your birth name is Alyxandretta Dagmar. Your parents were Alexi and Siobhan Dagmar."

She froze, one hand on the passenger side door. Daniel stared at her steadily and held up his hand as he ticked off the information.

"Your father's father and his father before him were born in Norway, the grandson and son respectively of the Grand Duchess Elizabeta Dagmar of Russia and first cousin to the Czar Nicholas II." He didn't smirk. If anything, he sounded resigned.

"So?" Alyx could have bitten her tongue for

interrupting when he went silent for a long moment.

"She was his only surviving relative and potential heir following the Czar's execution in 1917. Yes, I know that women couldn't inherit *but* she was one of the only direct heirs. Your family was —*is* one of the wealthiest in Europe. The grand duchess fled Russia for Norway the night of the coup, barely making it across the border. Her husband was not as fortunate. Her son, Nicolai— named for her beloved cousin—was just four years old." Daniel stepped forward and took her ignored coffee cup off the top of the car. "They were offered asylum by their family in Norway and remained there until your grandfather immigrated to the United States."

Slack-jawed, she stared at him. She wasn't certain what was more startling. The story or the ring of truth she heard in his voice.

Get in the car, Alyx.

But she didn't open the door. The picture he painted with staccato facts echoed barely remembered fairy tales from her childhood. She recognized the names from vague memories of best-forgotten bedtime stories her father used to tell her.

"How do you know that?" Her father had always called her princess, but he'd worked as an accountant and her mother a schoolteacher. They'd lived in a pretty little yellow house for as long as she could remember. Papa had mowed the lawn. Mama had planted flowers. Alyx had played in the cracked driveway, drawing hop-scotch with chalk.

At least she had before they died. A bad patch of ice and a drunk driver shattered her childhood. She'd been left with a single suitcase of clothes and an Imperial teddy bear that currently lay on the floor of her car. If she'd had any family at all, they would have come for her.

But they hadn't.

"I know this because you're a popular urban legend—well, your father was. His father lost all of his investments to bad gambling debts and a propensity for alcohol. His family cut him off, and he ran away to America to remake his fortune and they lost track of him. Rumors circulated in inner circles speculated about his son and his grand-daughter. But they were dismissed as rumors. Until now."

Rumors. Why did he have to sound like he believed this bedtime story? Sure... *She* was a princess. A princess with four years of college debt, low prospects and an acting career on the fast track to nowhere. Hell, she slept in her ten-year-old Volvo because it was all she could afford. "Look, I appreciate that you think you've hit the mother lode. But I don't have any money. I sure as hell don't have a title, and I wouldn't know a grand duke if I tripped over him on the street—thanks for the titillating story, but no, thanks."

Thinking about her parents made her nos-talgic for those mornings when she'd woken up and run into their room to bounce on the bed. Or better, the breakfasts her mother had insisted on cooking every morning and the way her father would slide his hands around her mother's waist and hug her from behind before twirling her into a dance.

Grief fisted around her heart.

She missed them.

Every day she missed them. She'd seen happily ever after.

And worse, she'd seen what happened after the last page of the fairy tale. She didn't want to think about it now.

Daniel sighed and took two steps forward, but remained on the other side of the vehicle. "I don't think you have any money, Pri—Miss Dagmar. But I do. A lot of money. More money than I could ever spend. I want to give you money. I want to help you claim the title and position that you should always have had."

"All so I can help you get your software company access to EU markets?" Skepticism poured thick on the words. No one did anything for nothing. And he was asking her to believe he just wanted her name—a name that frankly didn't mean anything.

She'd gone to school with a man named Brad Pitt—he didn't benefit from sharing the actor's moniker and heaven knew neither did Tina Fay, who was only one letter off. Just having the right name wasn't a game changer, particularly in her case. No one had heard of her—yet. She planned to change that. All she needed was the right part, the right role, and she could launch her acting career. Until then it was nights at

Roughy's Steakhouse and days at lessons and auditions.

"Exactly. It's a more than fair and equitable trade." His mouth compressed, frustration knitting his brows together. It added a darker, more attractive layer of intensity—and he wore it well. Her stomach clenched and she was glad that a car separated them. She'd never been attracted to insanity before and this didn't seem like the best time to get started.

Reaching into a pocket, Daniel pulled out a card and slid it across the roof of the vehicle. "Think about it. I have all the proof at my attorney's office—including copies of your birth certificate, the obituary for your grandfather, photographs of your great-grandparents and a detailed report from the private investigator I hired."

That gave her a jolt. She stared at the card like it was a snake—or worse, an apple from a snake. Talk about an invasion of privacy.

"Can you do that? Can you think about it?" His fingers were steady on the card's edge and his gaze compelling. She made the mistake of staring into those too-blue eyes. Her gut said she could trust him, but her mind shrieked like a bad heroine racing away from an axe murderer in a horror movie.

Nothing good ever came from trusting a stranger.

But he didn't seem to be going anywhere. She fisted the Taser in right hand, ready to zap if he did anything funny, and reached for the card.

Her fingers brushed the edge, but he didn't let it go.

"Call me. Anytime. I'll meet you anywhere you want. Anywhere you feel safe." The words unlocked the band of suspicion winding around her chest.

"Okay. I'll think about it and I'll take your card." The admission cost her nothing and promised even less. *Thinking* about it was *not* a commitment.

He nodded and let go of the card, watching until she picked it up. But he didn't leave, standing there and staring at her.

"Princess, I know you think I'm crazy and maybe I am. But if you do this for me, I can promise you, you won't regret it." Shivers chased over her skin at the quiet, solemn oath. He gave her a tight smile and a little salute, and then finally retreated to his black Lexus. She said nothing, watching him slide into the driver's seat. The engine rumbled to life with a smooth purr and he donned sunglasses before backing the vehicle out.

She watched him until the car disappeared around the curve and descended into the garage. Fingering the card, she padded over to the wall and glanced down the six stories to the street below. Two minutes later, his Lexus pulled out and turned onto La Cienega and blended into morning traffic.

Surprising herself, she looked down at the card. She should crumple it up and throw it away. That was what logic and common sense told her to do. But she wanted coffee—she opened the door and tucked the card up under her sun visor. Climbing back into the car, she put her keys in the ignition and started the engine. No way in hell could she contemplate sleep at this garage—not after her visitor and his wild proposition. Her mind hummed with the possibilities of it all, but it didn't matter.

Fairy tales weren't made of common sense and logic—they were leaps of faith.

CHAPTER 2
DANIEL

Stupid. Impulsive. Dumbass. Daniel smacked his hand against the steering wheel. *What the hell were you thinking?* He wanted to yell, not like anyone would notice. They would think he was just like every other dick driving in L.A. traffic. But it wasn't traffic that'd tied him up in knots, it was the look of utter confusion and refusal on the princess's face that did it.

He shouldn't have approached her at the car, but the impulse to follow her from the restaurant the night before had been too strong to resist. It didn't hurt that the private investigator he'd hired reported that she slept in her car. Believing that to be a mistake, he'd followed her into the garage and up to the near top, parking around the corner. He waited to see her leave via the stairs or the elevator, but when two hours passed without a sign of her, he'd driven the rest of the way up.

Sure enough, she was not only in her car, she was sound asleep in the back. He'd pulled up next to her, thinking the engine would rouse her.

When that didn't, he'd sat there for nearly an hour on that empty desolate parking garage roof. The sexy redhead was exposed, choosing to rest in such an insecure location. Leaving to go get the coffee had been an impulse, but he couldn't get the image of her in her car—alone—out of his head. He'd ordered the extra coffee and croissants and decided on a bonehead maneuver.

"I toss making a reasonable approach for coffee and end up scaring the shit out of her. Brilliant move, Voldakov, brilliant." Not that his plan didn't have its flaws, he'd just asked a stranger to move in and marry him five minutes after waking her up. Her white-knuckled grip on the Taser had never relaxed. Why the hell would it?

His body tightened at the memory of her sleep-rumpled face, tousled hair and husky voice. It didn't matter that she'd rolled out of a backseat and not his bed, he knew exactly what he wanted from her right then and it had nothing to do with contracts, access, or bloodlines.

He tapped his fingers against the steering wheel. He should call his attorney. He was likely to be facing a harassment suit. Not that she would be wrong. Of course, maybe she would just get a restraining order. "Penniless Princess takes out restraining order against CEO—news at eleven."

But she's living in her car.

That single fact tumbled around and around in his brain. He hadn't really believed the PI's report—or his own eyes—when he saw her sleeping in the car until he got a good look at the supplies stored inside. Clothes, blankets, pillow and a ratty stuffed bear missing one eye.

The damn bear got to him.

What good would it do to call him now? He needed *plan*, but he struggled to focus on the drive. He'd put his foot in it. No mistaking that, but he could recover the situation. She needed help. He had help to offer. The exchange could be advantageous to both of them.

Or you can just suck it up and let your products speak for themselves.

Spherecast developed top-of-the-line software and had rapidly climbed as the go-to company for corporate network security and intrusion prevention. His reputation in the States was impeccable and he'd developed strong contacts and even better contracts, including a near billion dollar one that would launch them throughout South America. But Europe continued to elude him. It wasn't that the software didn't work; on the contrary, it performed brilliantly. The design prevented hackers from access by turning tunnels back on themselves or leading them through into trap algorithms. The programs then automatically recorded incoming packet locations and waited for specific handoff signals, and if they weren't received—well, the resulting virus the hacker got back was nasty. Penetrating the old guard of networking connections that dated back to lords and their serfs held him firmly at bay. Then there was the EU itself. They protected their own resources and had some of the strictest laws with regards to internet protocols and privacy.

The Andrastes offered him the best opportunity for corporate synergy. They had the connections, the pedigree, and even better, they were already established there. He'd tried the direct approach with the Andraste family and slammed up against stone wall after stone wall—most he'd been able to trace back to the grand duke's legal team.

He'd carved out a niche for his company, investing in his own skills and reinvesting in the talent that worked for him. They were the *best*. The lack of title shouldn't keep him shut out of Europe. Not when his damn product was the best thing out there. But the old guard didn't see it that way. His Bolshevik roots probably didn't help. But the Voldakovs were three generations deep in the US and he barely understood the Russian his grandmother had sung to lull him to sleep. Parking, he swallowed his temper and headed for the elevator. Dwelling on what hadn't worked wouldn't get him anywhere. He needed a plan.

Okay, I need a new plan...

Arriving at the office ahead of his staff wasn't that unusual. He took the time to trade his shirt for a fresh one he stored in the bottom of his desk and checked the ties in the drawer above it for one without a stain. His secretary, Lucy, was fantastic about these things.

Settling in behind his desk, he flipped open the folder the P.I. delivered the day before. Photographs of Alyx spilled out, digital time stamps giving him a good idea of her schedule. She worked most evenings at the restaurant—where he'd first set eyes on her—and she split her daytime hours between auditions and classes.

When she's not sleeping in her car.

If not for his mother's passion for all things royal and the umpteen gajillion documentaries and news programs she watched about all of them, he might never have made the connection. But one only had to look at Alyx to see the family resemblance. He'd dined there three nights in a row trying to figure out where he'd seen her before, and it was only by accident that a news bite on the grand duke late one night helped him put the pieces together. The facial structures were strikingly similar. The rich, vibrance of her deep red hair might be more vivid than the rest of the family, but it fit. Her jaw was softer and rounder, but the eyes—they could have been twins.

He would never be sure which idea occurred first—hiring the investigator or coughing up some royal blood to grease the wheels. Martin cracked a joke about borrowing a title to get their foot in the door. If it hadn't been for another frustrating series of stalls on the EU inspector's part, he might have just asked her out on a date. *Hell, I still want to ask her out on a date...*

Picking up the phone, he dialed his attorney's number. Martin answered on the first ring.

"Martin Grange."

"I spoke to her this morning," he began without preamble.

"Oh, for the love of God, Daniel. We talked about this. Are you in jail? Do I need to come bail you out?" Martin was definitely not on board with his idea. In fact, his attorney labeled it foolish and told him to just play on the up-and-up. It would take them time to make their mark, but by then, the European companies would be coming to him—not the other way around.

"No. I'm at the office." He toyed with the pen on the desk and drew a squiggly line down the center of the blank legal pad. On the right side he wrote pros and the left, he wrote cons. "She wasn't thrilled with the opportunity."

"You sound surprised." Martin, however, did not.

"She's sleeping out of her car." He wrote *needs a home* under pro. "Her car. She parks it at the top of a public parking garage off La Cienega and climbs in the back to go to sleep. She has no security. Just takes one whackjob to knock out her windows and she's in trouble."

"That's her choice. You know, there are plenty of shelters out there for the homeless and it's not like she doesn't have a job. She works at one of the swankiest steakhouses in Beverly Hills. She has to make three to four hundred a night."

Daniel added dollar signs under the pro column along with two question marks. If she did make that much in tips, then why didn't she have a place of her own? Apartments in L.A. were expensive, but she could find one in North Hollywood for about a week's worth of tips. It would be small, but her car was hardly a palace. "Exactly. The report says she went to the University of California on scholarships, but the three she received couldn't have covered all of her tuition and her housing—that means student loans."

Martin sighed. "Daniel, stop. You rescue puppies in the pouring rain when you're wearing a five-thousand-dollar suit. Not to mention what wet dog smell does to a Lamborghini. Just let this go."

"That was my Lexus, not the Lamborghini. And the detailer got the smell out and the dog got a home." *Needs help.* He wrote that down beneath the pros *and* circled it. He studied the list—two items on the pros and none on the cons did not make a fair argument.

"Has the grand duke returned any of our calls?" They'd been courting Andraste for months, subtly. They'd used connections and parties to try to get closer to the man, but the grand duke's entourage was not easily penetrated. Getting access to him proved more difficult than finding Willy Wonka's golden ticket. It irked the hell out of Daniel that his "new" money bourgeois didn't merit a call above receptionist.

"No, but that's not a reason to—"

Daniel's cell phone rang and he glanced down at it. Only three people had that number. His secretary never called him before nine and Martin was on the phone. "Martin, I have to go. She's calling."

"Daniel, wait—" But he hung up on his attorney's protests and thumbed the answer button on the cell.

"Hello?"

"Daniel Voldakov?" Her husky voice sounded smoother, more alert.

"Hello, Princess." He leaned back in the chair and turned around to look out the window. He couldn't see the parking garage from his vantage, but he could imagine her yellow tank top, white shorts and long tan legs.

"Why don't you just call me Alyx and skip the whole royal shtick, okay?" Impatience crept into her voice. Impatience and if he wasn't mistaken, curiosity.

"All right, Alyx. If you want me to call you that."

"I do."

He nodded, though she couldn't see him. "Done. See, I'm a reasonable man. I take it you've thought about my offer." He'd imagined it would take her longer. Worried really.

"Yes. I wasn't going to call. In fact, I was just going to throw out your card, but since you did bring me coffee, I figured I owed you a little courtesy."

Damn.

"It's a no, then?" He pursed his lips and glanced back at the file about her.

"Exactly. Thanks for the thought."

"You're very welcome."

"Goodbye, Mr. Voldakov."

"Until next time, Miss Dagmar." He listened to the distinct pause as his words sank in. When the phone clicked off, he picked up the P.I.'s report. She wanted to be an actress.

Switching to his desktop phone, he dialed his secretary's number. "Lucy."

"Mr. Voldakov, it's not nine. You know the rules." The older woman had been with him since he opened his first business out of his garage. A family neighbor for thirty years, she was the only one who could get away with talking to him like that.

And she never called him Mr. Voldakov unless he annoyed her.

"I'll put a ten-dollar bill in your candy jar as soon as I hang up." He also didn't mind paying the penalty fee. She kept candy for all the employees' kids when they visited and more for her own grandchildren, and he paid a fine for every out-of-office-hours call.

It worked for them.

"All right, what can I do for you?"

"What do you know about advertising for an actress?"

THREE DAYS LATER, he leaned back in the auditorium of the theater he'd rented for the day. His secretary'd placed an advertisement in all the papers for a casting call. They'd listed very specific qualities and appearance. He'd gone through every resume and photograph that arrived until he found Alyx Dagmar's.

She was the only one he wanted, and she was the only one who made the cut.

He wrote the script himself. It was a bastardized version of *My Fair Lady*, but he didn't care. The names and the places were all that mattered—well, and the princess in question.

The theater crew admitted her, gave her access to a dressing room and the pages she would cold read for the part. Right on schedule she walked out on the stage. He knew she couldn't see him in the darkened theater.

Clasping his hands together, he sat back and watched as she took her spot. "Whenever you're ready." He called quietly, certain it would carry.

"Good evening, ladies and gentlemen." She lifted her hand as though holding a glass up to make a toast. Dressed in the simple green strapless gown, with her glorious ruby hair pinned up, she seemed as glamorous as any model. "It is time for us to remove our masks, to reveal ourselves to each other in the fine tradition of the old-world masquerade. Have you danced with a duke? Did you dine with a princess? Did you discover your true love?"

She flowed three steps toward the lip of the stage, the single spotlight highlighting the magnificent column of her throat. He held his breath. She was better than he imagined. With all the gesture of flourish she mimed the removal of a mask. Her smile lit up her face and he leaned forward.

An air of expectancy hung around her, cloaking her as her smile turned coy, secretive. The notes said she was to react to surprise with a hint of delight. But the riot of emotion she let play over her face captivated him.

With a graceful curtsy, she dipped toward the stage and her gaze roved over the audience. He could almost imagine she hunted for him in the shadows and when she paused to straighten, her chin came up. "Yes," she said in a clear, true voice. "My name is Princess D'tente."

It was a stupid name, he grimaced at it, but he'd wanted her to take the message in it.

"And at long last, I am reunited with my family." She paused again, but this wasn't in the script. Her smile faltered and fell away.

Her gaze arrowed straight at him, where he sat, arms braced on the back of the seat in front of him.

"You son of a bitch."

Yep. That definitely wasn't in the script.

CHAPTER 3
ALYX

L ivid, Alyx stormed down the steps, stage right. Everything about the audition had seemed a bit odd, from the part advertised, to just how closely the description fit her. But she'd hoped—really, prayed—that this would be the breakout part for her. Even if it wasn't, stage time could be invaluable and give her weeks of developing a rapport with an audience.

Still, warning bells rang when she'd arrived and found no one else prepping to audition. The red-alert klaxon went off when she scanned the lines they wanted her to perform for the cold reading. A princess, found again, making a splashy entrance to society via a masquerade ball.

The stage lights hid Daniel from her, but as her eyes adjusted and he leaned forward, she recognized the man's silhouette. It belonged to the idiot knocking on her car window. How she made it down the stairs without tripping in the uncomfortable heels, she didn't know, but she strode up the aisle toward him on a wave of righteous fury and indignation.

"Miss Dagmar, before you tear into me—as you have every right to do—let me tell you that you were absolutely magnificent. You wear the role of princess like you were born to it." His compliments failed to dull the rage boiling in her belly.

"How dare you?" She paused to gather her breath and shook with the outrage coursing in her veins. "How dare you play a game with my career? I took time off from my *job* to come down here and perform a farce."

"Actually, you took time off to answer an audition call. I didn't twist your arm. I made that listing very specific and you are perfect for the part." He met her ire with utter calmness.

It only served to infuriate her more.

"There is no part, is there?" *Dammit.* She'd needed tonight's tips for the immersion class. Now she would have to reschedule because she wouldn't have enough by Friday. *Stupid. Stupid. Stupid.* She should have trusted her instincts, but the part sounded wonderful and she couldn't wait to wear the clothes and transform herself.

All for a lie.

"There is a part. The same part I told you about." Wow, the man just did not give up. "A part you were *born* to play."

Bowing her head and hands on her hips, she fought to get her breathing and temper under control. To her horror, tears actually burned in her eyes and she blinked furiously to keep them back. She would not break down in front of the hunk with the crackpot offer. "I told you no. I said thanks, but no thanks. What part of that answer are you having trouble with?"

"All of it." He shifted, leaning a hip against an aisle chair and releasing her from the tension of his nearness. A tension she'd failed to notice until he gave her the space to breathe. "Alyx, I can make things happen in your world. I can change it and you can change mine. It's an equitable deal."

"I don't know you and so far, what I've learned hasn't impressed me." *Liar.* The advertisement for the audition was an act of pure genius. Despite her anger, she couldn't help but be flattered.

"Then get to know me. Meet my attorney. Look at my bank statements. Come to my office. I am exactly who I say I am and I *need* your help for exactly the reasons I've described." He leaned forward, the darkness of the theater framing his earnest expression. "You have nothing to lose and everything to gain."

"Why?" *Why am I not just walking away from this guy? Why do his eyes seem to say he is telling the truth?* She didn't have answers to her own questions, much less why he wanted *her.*

"Because you *are* a princess. If you need proof, I have that too."

Need proof? Yeah, she needed proof.

Was she actually considering doing this? She rubbed a hand against her cheek, turning to look across the empty seats. Leaving seemed the safest bet, but the lengths he went to just to get her in this theater...

"Alyx. You live out of your car. I hate that. If nothing else, let me pay you for the time it takes to consider the idea. Enough to get you a place to live." Contrition and hope struggled in those sentences and she forgave him for the deception. Maybe just a little bit.

"What's the name of your attorney?"

He straightened, a smile flaring briefly to life on his lips. "Martin Grange. He's a partner at Grange, Dubbin and Grange. His number is—"

"Stop." She held up a hand. "I'll get the number. You stay here." With as much grace as she could muster, she spun on a heel and strode to the stage, up the steps and through the wings to the dressing room where she'd left her phone. She glanced back—checking his location twice before she went into the wings. Daniel stayed right where she bid him.

She googled the information and looked up a number for the law firm. Waiting to be connected, she glanced at herself in the mirror and shook her head. "Dreamer."

"Grange, Dubbin and Grange. How may I direct your call?"

"Martin Grange, please." She slipped off the heels and put the cell phone on speaker while the receptionist transferred her.

Another woman came on the line. "Martin Grange's office."

"Yes, I would like to speak to Mr. Grange. My

name is Alyx Dagmar." She unzipped the dress and stripped it off—trading the expensive costume for capris and a clean tank top. She'd stopped at the fitness club next to the restaurant that morning. A regular customer managed the location and let her use the showers for free when they weren't crowded.

"May I tell him what this is in regards to?"

"Daniel Voldakov." *Voldakov*. It sounded Russian. The name, not the man. Perching on the edge of a chair, she stuffed her feet into her sandals.

"This is Martin Grange." A question hung suspended amid the statement.

Alyx picked up the phone and thumbed off the speaker before putting it to her ear. "Mr. Grange, my name is Alyx Dagmar. I wanted to ask you some questions about Daniel Voldakov."

"All right." The attorney kept his tone neutral, but wary.

"First, is he your client?" She dragged her purse over and fished past the pepper spray and Taser for lip gloss.

"Yes, I represent Mr. Voldakov. If you are planning a nuisance suit, I can assure you that won't be necessary. We can settle this amicably." The man sounded aggrieved.

"I'm not planning anything at the moment. Would you describe Mr. Voldakov to me?" She didn't bother to disguise the bite in her tone. He'd already admitted to representing her blond stalker. Applying the gloss, she checked her teeth and studied her appearance. She didn't wear much makeup to conserve her supplies. It rankled that she wasted some for this fake audition.

"Mr. Voldakov is about six foot one, blond hair, blue eyes. He has a small circular scar at the corner of his right eye. Is he there currently?"

Heh. Looks like his attorney isn't thrilled with him either.

"He's in the theater." She zipped up the purse and slung it over her shoulder. "Does Mr. Voldakov actually own a software company?"

"He does. Spherecast Technologies."

"And he's raking in the bucks stateside but can't make it in the European market?" She followed the hallway to backstage and through a side door into the audience. Daniel stood exactly where she'd left him, arms folded across his broad chest. The frown wrinkling his brow smoothed when she appeared.

"I'm not comfortable discussing Mr. Voldakov's finances with you, Miss Dagmar."

"Fair enough. Are you aware of the proposal he made to me?" She walked up the aisle, aware that Daniel could hear her. A muscle ticked in his jaw.

"I am. I apologize for his enthusiasm, but he genuinely means well."

"Does he? And this investigation he did into my background, did he go through your office?" She stood in front of Daniel, meeting his gaze defiantly.

"Again, I'm going to have to decline to discuss Mr. Voldakov's private affairs with you."

The corner of her mouth quirked. The attorney's annoyance had focused on her instead of his client. She put him on speaker and held the phone out so Daniel could hear. "I'm with Mr. Voldakov now, Mr. Grange."

"Daniel?"

"I'm here. Tell the lady whatever she needs to know."

"I think we should discuss this further. Why don't we make an appointment?" The poor man really did not care for being put on the spot, but she kept her gaze firmly on Daniel, looking for any sign of deception or avoidance.

"No. Just answer her questions." *Point to Daniel.*

"Very well. Yes, Mr. Voldakov's company is facing stress from competitors to access the right permits and licenses to sell in the European Union." Nope, the attorney wasn't one little bit happy.

"Is it because of the product or is he trying to shortcut his way through regulations?" She lifted her eyebrows as Daniel cocked his head, a mild look of incredulity on his face. Yes, she did have an education and wasn't afraid to use it.

"Regulations aren't the issue precisely. Approval from the conglomerates that control the regulatory bodies are. They negotiate on a social and economic basis. We won't have problems meeting the technical specifications or economic necessities."

A ghost of a smile flirted on Daniel's lips. The attorney confirmed his earlier story about needing social access.

"And if he is engaged to a princess?" The question just didn't taste right, but she forced it out anyway.

"Then, yes, we could very well have social capital to negotiate with." She and the attorney were on the same wavelength. He sounded less enthusiastic about the idea than she. He cleared his throat. "Or at least to open the doors to those conversations." So it wasn't a home run, but it would get him up to bat.

"Thank you, Mr. Grange."

"Miss Dagmar. Daniel, I'll be calling you shortly." The attorney hung up and Alyx laughed.

"I think he's mad at you." She pocketed the phone.

"Probably. I make his life hell some days. Do you believe me?" He'd uncrossed his arms while she talked to Martin and tucked his hands into the pockets of his khaki pants. If not for the expensive shirt and equally expensive shoes, he looked like a man ready to take a walk on a sandy beach.

"Honestly? I don't know. It still sounds ridiculous. You have no idea what kind of a person I am and I haven't any idea what kind of a person you are, other than you make outlandish offers and go to some extreme lengths to have your case heard." Which was a little bit romantic, but she wasn't about to tell him that. Romantic or insane, at the moment she wasn't seeing a lot of difference. Adjusting the grip on her purse, she shrugged. "And even if I believed you and your intentions, this is all based on the supposition that I'm actually a princess. Which I'm not. I don't care what your proof says I am..." She spread her hands out, the last line a lie, but he didn't need to know it. "I don't know how to be one. I grew up in Sonoma and Sacramento. I went to public school. I lived in foster homes. I can make a mean burger and memorize a hundred-item menu, but those aren't exactly princess-level skills."

"You can learn to be a princess. You can learn the walk, the talk and the manners. You're the *lost* princess, after all. No one will expect you be perfect. That's all window dressing, anyway. We can't manufacture a lineage. But *you* have that."

However impossible, it didn't sound improbable. She leaned against a seat and folded her arms. "How long?"

He didn't quite grin. "At least six months, a year would be better. Engagements take a lot of time and we'll both need time to learn how to act and to get our manners and mannerisms down."

A year.

She rubbed her forehead. A year was a hell of a long time. That was a lot of classes to miss and her job...

"I can pay you for every hour of every day you spend on this. You're going to help me secure a multi-billion-dollar deal. You're going to get a publicity blitz like you've never experienced, and name recognition. That's golden capital in the acting world. Consider for a moment that you'll have front-page access, network news—domestic and international. You can't buy the kind of stardom this will net for you." He ticked off the items on his fingers. "You can have all of that, secure your future acting career. Name your price, it's yours."

"That's awfully blasé and open ended. I need to think about the money, and the time, and we're going to need a legally binding contract— one that draws it all out in black and white." Could they even *enforce* a contract like that? This wasn't just taking a role, this was going to take every hour of my life.

Still, anticipation thrummed through her at the mention of name recognition. He wasn't wrong. She didn't merit a blip on the radar yet, just another pretty face with a too-thin resume and a lot of audition experience. This could change absolutely everything. Like a reverse Grace Kelly or something.

"Anything." His grin grew. "We can go see Martin right now and start hammering out the deal."

"I need a few days to wrap my mind around this." *And to talk myself out of this. Is his madness contagious?* "I also want to see this proof you have about my family."

"I'll bring it to the restaurant. But a few days? You're still going to be in your car." His brow crinkled. "Why don't I set you up at the Beverly Hills Hilton? It's not far from the restaurant. You can have the time and the security to review everything."

"The car thing really bothers you, doesn't it?"

She didn't get it. They were strangers. So what if she slept in her car?

"A lady shouldn't have to sleep in her car."

"I'll be fine. Just drop the folder off at the restaurant and I'll pick it up. I can call you in a few days." *Maybe by then I'll have located my sanity again.*

"Can I buy you dinner? Coffee? I'll book the room at the Hilton—if you change your mind, just go by and they'll have a room key for you." He wasn't going to let that go.

"Mr. Voldakov, I'm considering your proposal. Maybe I'll marry you, maybe I won't. That is just going to have to be enough. But when a lady says she needs to think about it, piece of advice, let her think."

He held out his hand. "Three days?"

"Sure, why not." She huffed a breath and took his hand. Shock raced up her arm and set her pulse tingling. He smiled, squeezing her hand gently, and her heart hitched at the breathtaking grin.

"You won't regret it. I promise."

We'll see about that.

CHAPTER 4
ALYX

"**A**re you seriously considering his offer?" Rhonda sat on the edge of the picnic table bench, a cigarette dangling between two fingers. The restaurant opened in an hour, they were set up and they had some time to kill. Nestled among the trees and bushes, the smoking area was deserted save for the two of them. Alyx didn't smoke, but she wanted to take advantage of the rare quiet time to chat without interruptions.

"I don't know." She sighed. In the two days since the theater fiasco, Daniel, his offer, his blue eyes and what accepting all of the above would be like were the only things she had thought about. As promised, an envelope containing her family research arrived at the restaurant the next day. It sat unopened in her car.

"You *are* considering it." Standing, Rhonda shook her head, looking around as if to ascertain they were alone, then stared at her. "You don't know this guy. He could be some kind of crackpot and his attorney an accomplice—if the guy was really an attorney."

"He was. I googled Martin Grange and looked him up via the California Bar Association. I found photos and news articles about him. Did the same for Daniel. They're real. They are who they say they are." Which made the conundrum muckier than it already was. What the hell did it say about them that they wanted to use fraud—well, not fraud, not if he was right about her. But weren't they asking for an act? An illusion to make a business deal happen?

"You didn't meet the attorney, sweetie. You talked to him on the phone." Her friend grimaced.

"No, I didn't see him but he was in captioned in a photograph with Daniel last year. The photo matched his bar association page." Stretching, she paced away from the table and the haze of smoke. Too many possibilities crowded in her mind. Her gut twisted with indecision. She told him no at the parking garage. While the audition didn't completely reverse her decision, she sat firmly on the fence between the risky promise of the unknown and the less certain success of the road she traveled.

"Do you hear yourself? You're thinking about —" Rhonda glanced around again, dropping her voice to a whisper, "—getting engaged to a guy you don't know and walking away from your life to play a *part*."

"But isn't that kind of what I always wanted to do? Be an actress, play a role, inhabit the part?"

"On. Stage." Her friend crushed the cigarette out and snapped her fingers in front of Alyx's face. "Wake up. This isn't a part—this is your life."

We're going to have to learn the mannerisms and manners...

I'll hire someone to teach us how to do it...

You were born for this part...

"Rhonda, I'm going to do it."

The bottle blonde sighed and pulled her hair back into a ponytail. "I knew you would. You are the most daring, adventurous, out-of-her-mind person I know. You see something you want, you go after it. You live out of your car, you shower in a gym and you're still together and on top of things. Me, I do good for the day by day. You? See the mountain, take the mountain."

"Tell me how you really feel." She grinned. Rhonda was her oldest friend in Los Angeles and the reason she got the job at the steakhouse in the first place. Rhonda'd tried to talk her into sharing her apartment, but it was too cramped with Rhonda and her boyfriend. She did, however, sublet the guest room closet for her nicer outfits so they didn't get crumpled in the car.

The older woman took her by the shoulders and stared at her. "You get everything in writing and you get some of that money up front. You also remember you have an out—anything gets hinky, you come straight to me." Pursing her lips, she shook her head slowly. "I still think you should just say forget it. You have the information. If you want to track down your royal roots, you don't need this guy."

"It's not about that." And curiously enough, it wasn't. She'd gotten used to having no family. She'd had sixteen years of getting used to it. Some days, she couldn't picture what her mom and dad looked like. She remembered how they smelled—her mother'd loved Tabu perfume and her father'd favored Old Spice. If she closed her eyes and concentrated, she could almost imagine the feeling of their hugs, but that was it. Capturing those elusive moments was one the reasons she liked sleeping in her car. Some her best memories were falling asleep in the backseat on the way back from some adventure while her parents talked in the front seat.

On really bad days, she could close her eyes, hug her bear and soak up that feeling.

"Then why?" Rhonda tilted her head, expression curious and concerned, but lacking judgment. "Why take this kind of leap?"

"Because it's crazy. It's—immersion. It's becoming someone else entirely. If I can do *this*, then I really do have a future in acting. It's not just some fairytale I dreamed up one night to run away from a foster home."

"Sweetheart, this isn't just *immersion* like you're playing a part in a movie. This is the real thing and you're talking about marrying a guy you don't know?"

"I'm not actually marrying him." She went over his request so many times in the past two days she'd memorized it. He wanted an engagement. He wanted a splashy showing. He didn't say they had to go through with it. Catching Rhonda close in a quick hug, she grinned. "It's going to be fine. I'll make sure I have the parachute on before I jump."

"I worry about you," Rhonda said, utterly unconvinced. "You need to check in with me and regularly. I want to know he hasn't buried you in his backyard or locked you up in his cellar or something."

She made a face. "That's a cheery thought."

"It's a realistic one. You're usually a lot more practical than this." Dislike kissed every single word.

"Then I promise, I'll check in and text you regularly." It wouldn't be a bad thing to have someone know where she was. "I'll make sure you have the address too."

"Good. Take selfies to, I want to be able to see that you're fine." She shook her head. "If you change your mind at *any* point, one phone call, fuck it, just show up. You can come to me."

That helped. Maybe more than she knew. Alyx hugged her again. "Thank you." Even if she didn't like it, didn't want her doing it, she wasn't cutting ties.

After Rhonda went inside, she pulled out her cell and the crinkled business card. She weighed the decision for another minute before dialing the number. She could have texted it, but this seemed like something where it would be better if they spoke.

"Okay," she committed. "I'm in."

~

DANIEL

Daniel controlled the urge to fidget as she read through the papers. Martin stood in the center of the salon-style room with Daniel perched on the edge of a chair while she sat on the sofa opposite.

She took her time scanning the contract, reading each page—sometimes twice. Occasionally she circled something, the faint crinkle of the paper and the scritch of the pen the only sounds in the room. On the last page was the amount he'd told Martin to write in. He already had a check drawn.

"No." Alyx shook her head, jerking her attention from the paper.

"It's a more than equitable amount." Martin intervened before Daniel could answer.

"It's five million dollars. That's way too much." She leaned back, the papers a neat stack on her lap.

Daniel glanced at his attorney and saw a perplexed expression that mirrored his own confusion. They'd expected she might ask for more, but less?

"I'm asking you to commit to this project twenty-four hours a day, seven days a week for a year. I don't think five million is too much for that kind of investment." He kept his voice calm, but he couldn't keep the question out of it.

"It's too much. Look, I work six nights a week at the steakhouse. I make about three

42

hundred a day, average. Some days are better, some are worse, but six days a week for fifty two weeks is sixty-two thousand four hundred dollars, after taxes. Five million is way too much."

"You want us to *reduce* the amount of payment?" Martin folded his arms, his frown turning speculative.

"Yes. I also want half up front. In addition, I want you to set up a scholarship fund for foster kids in California—discretionary aid to help them pay for college. If you want to invest five million, then take—I don't know—set one million aside for me and put the rest in the scholarship fund." She tapped the paper. "I also want an open-ended round-trip ticket to anywhere in the world, dated for one year from today. And an apartment. In my name—here in the city, and I'm the only one with keys to it."

Clasping his hands together, Daniel leaned forward. "Alyx, the scholarship fund isn't a problem." Martin cleared his throat, but Daniel ignored him. "But I think you should take more than just a million. I get that you think it's too much, but realistically—a million goes fast. What about the rest of your life?"

She shrugged. "What about it? I don't have a house. If you pay one year of an apartment for me —it's a done deal, no rent payments. I'm not going to have that job anymore and I'm assuming you're going to feed me—that won't be an expense. I can put the half you pay me up front in the bank, it can collect interest, and one year from today I collect the other half and I can get on a plane and go anywhere I want."

"And you're willing to sign a waiver to relieve Mr. Voldakov of any other financial remuneration associated with this year?" His attorney studied her, seeming as uncertain as Daniel was of her counteroffer.

"Yes. He's paying for whatever lessons, clothes—" she flipped through the pages, "—travel and anything else required to deliver on the idea that I am a princess. I won't have to spend anything. Maybe we can add a caveat that I keep the clothes— Oh, and no sex. I'm an actress, not a prostitute. I want that in the contract."

The hard look on her face surprised the hell out of him. She'd made a similar statement in one of their earlier meetings, but it hadn't occurred to him to add a sex clause and his body tightened in rebellion of the idea. Sex wasn't a requirement, but he hadn't dismissed the idea entirely. She was attractive and they were going to be in close quarters for the next several months.

Okay, maybe that wasn't a bad idea.

"I don't think that will be a problem." Of course Martin didn't think it would be a problem. He wasn't the one signing the agreement.

"And that's it? Those are your only stipulations?"

"Pretty much." She nodded. "We're not actually getting married. The legal right to my name remains mine. And your property remains yours. I'll leave this charade with the experience, the clothes, the scholarship funds, the plane ticket and a tidy bank account. That's all I want."

"You realize you're not stipulating any of the jewelry, including the engagement ring?" He ignored Martin's huff of annoyance, because no matter what she thought or his attorney believed, a year of her life was worth a lot more than she realized. She wasn't listing the taxes on that income either, but he would take care of those.

"Engagement ring?" Her eyebrows climbed in surprise.

"You didn't think you would get one? I'm asking a princess to marry me. I'm thinking that calls for something fairly fat and definitely diamond." A solitaire would be the perfect type of elegant—not that he knew much about jewelry.

"I think I'm good. It's a symbol of our arrangement, not any real feelings." The casual dismissal of the ring irked him, but he didn't look too closely at that.

"Fine. Martin, I need you to amend the contract to reflect Alyx's requirements. She agrees to study everything she needs to know about being a princess, will maintain the role full-time with no asides for auditions or a return to the life beyond what we construct. When we're in public, we're a loving couple. We have fun, we smile and we stare longingly into each other's eyes. Any time we're in the house and the staff is present, we're also on. Now, my staff is part-time and here two or three days a week, but we *can't* slip. I don't care if anyone questions your lineage or where you've been all these years, because we have the truth on our side for that one. But we can't afford any questions about *us* as a couple."

"I know. We have to sell ourselves as the next great love story of all time before it becomes tabloid fodder for crash and burn. Celebrity couples do break up." Her lips twisted into a wry smile. "Just remember, no sex."

"If you can keep your hands to yourself—" he grinned, "—so can I."

Her gaze flicked over him like a cold spray of water. "That won't be a problem. Oh, and, Martin?" She glanced at the attorney. "I want evidence of the scholarship fund being set up and a cashier's check in hand before I sign the contract."

The attorney looked to Daniel for approval, then sighed when he nodded. "You realize you're both certifiable?"

Daniel laughed, surprised and pleased when Alyx joined him. "I would say we're a perfect pair."

"Hmm." Martin hedged his response. "I'll draw up the papers and the checks. I'll meet with you both in the morning." He snapped his briefcase closed and left, disapproval hovering in his wake.

"He *really* doesn't like this plan." Alyx propped her chin on her hand and stared after him.

Filling two glasses with wine, Daniel shrugged. "He doesn't have to be happy. He just has to do the job." Carrying the glasses over, he held one out to her. "A toast."

"Question first." She took the glass and shot him quizzical glance. He didn't miss the flash of indecision in her eyes. Buyer's remorse was always a problem—it was up to him to keep her calm until all the *t*'s were crossed and the *i*'s dotted.

"Okay. Shoot."

"Why the hell is this important to you? Five million? A pretend engagement to a virtual stranger? Stalking me? Setting up the elaborate audition? Now a contract that makes your attorney squeamish. That's a hell of a lot of overkill just to sell some software. So—why?" She held the wineglass, her gaze sharp and assessing.

Intelligence was an attractive thing in a woman. Even when it pinned him to the spot like a target on a dartboard. "Because my company is on the cutting edge of every major security software development of the last five years and I can't get a meeting with these people. They do business with their own kind, it's not what you know—it's who you know." The knowledge wore at him like an ill-fitting shoe and rubbed him raw. It didn't matter how innovative his work was—*he* wasn't good enough. "I'm going to be creative, get my foot in the door, and then my work will do the rest."

She pursed her lips and he worried he'd said too much, pushed too hard. "I get that."

Another surprise in a day filled with them. "Do you?"

Lifting her shoulders, she gave him a bitter-sweet smile. "I've been the kid on the outside. It sucks. So yeah, I get it."

Maybe she really did understand... He didn't want to pick at those wounds. Not when Martin didn't seem to grasp why it aggravated him to be blocked at every turn. But a company that didn't grow, that didn't expand, would eventually stagnate. To stay on the edge, he needed to push his boundaries everywhere.

"To new beginnings." He held his glass out.

She stared at him for a long moment. "And a successful ending."

"I'll drink to that." Their glasses clinked together and he washed down his uncertainties with the California white.

Seven days from first meeting to signed contract. It beat every other business deal, hands down.

Hopefully, it would be all the more successful.

CHAPTER 5
ALYX

Waking in the king size bed didn't get any easier. Four days and nights spent in Daniel's sprawling estate, occupying a bedroom easily twice the size of Rhonda's entire apartment, and she still jerked awake. She slept on the far right of the bed, closer to the door than the twelve feet of ceiling-to-floor windows looking out over the garden below. A six-foot dresser and nightstand lined the brick wall next to the bed and a desk and sofa sat along the opposite wall.

Sitting and pulling her knees to her chest, she rubbed the sleep from her face.

The weirdest part of the room, however, was the spiral staircase that extended upward to the deck on this side of the house. The patio or salon was for her exclusive use. Daniel promised that although his bedroom next door shared similar access to it, he would cede the area to her for privacy.

What the hell was I thinking? She stared

around the room, always a little lost for what to do when she woke in the palatial suite.

A knock on the door sent her scrambling off the bed and she pulled the comforter to her chest. "Come in."

Daniel stepped inside, carrying a tray with coffee and croissants. The man delivered it every morning, like clockwork. "Good morning." He always looked so put together and delicious, from the open collar of his button-down shirt to his pressed slacks and casual loafers. Even his hair didn't have the decency to be tousled.

She caught sight of herself in the mirror and immediately wished she hadn't. Her hair's natural curl took over when she slept—like Gremlins fed water after midnight—and turned spiky and stuck straight toward the ceiling.

"Morning," she mumbled, glad this was a job and not an actual date.

The first morning he brought coffee, she hadn't been able to muster a greeting. He'd strolled into the room with a knock, set the coffee on the nightstand and gave her that heart-stopping grin before sailing out again. The second morning, he'd brought the coffee and spent a minute waiting for her to get out of bed and accept it.

Yesterday, he'd joined her for coffee.

It wasn't that he was bad company. Far from it, actually. She just wasn't used to someone being cheerful in the a.m. She could care for a little less morning time, perhaps postponing it until after twelve.

He handed her the cup with a bemused look. "Maybe you should go to bed earlier."

Alyx was almost too tired to glare, but she tried, delivering it over the rim of the coffee cup. "I was only up late because you wanted me to memorize the family tree and then we had to watch those two documentaries about the Czar's descendants."

She would never admit to a certain amount of fascination, particularly on the pieces that referenced her grandfather. Nor would she engage him in another debate about whether the man her father called dad and the grand duchess's grandson were one and the same.

Daniel remained convinced—she had her doubts.

Better to let that argument lie.

"Okay. Well, drink your coffee and then take a shower and drink more coffee. Victor will be here this afternoon to have lunch with us and do the initial assessment of our coupledom."

Alyx sighed. *There ain't no such thing as a free lunch. Time to earn my paycheck.*

She walked away from him, coffee cup in hand, to look out the window. The garden formed a geometric pattern of colors. Landscaped around a koi pond, roses flourished, daisies occupied a section and row upon row of morning glories and impatiens formed the colorful border. The whole of it was surrounded by a white stone wall that matched the white stone brick of the house and profusions of white jasmine spilling down its sides.

But the best part was also the most solitary. A white-roofed gazebo set off in the corner offered sanctuary with a splash of vivid color with its blue-painted wood. A table and chairs sat beneath on the pavestones that made up its floor, but it remained lonely with no flowers or growth attached to it.

Maybe that was why she liked it.

"Alyx?"

"Do you ever go out there?" She glanced over her shoulder. Daniel studied something on his digital tablet.

"Where?"

"Out there, in the garden." She jerked a thumb toward the window. "Do you ever go out there?"

Daniel crossed the room and glanced outside, distraction evident in every gesture. "Not often. We held a launch party for some investors there last year. By the way, Victor wants us to make a list of what we'd find the most uncomfortable to do. I started one, I thought we could go over it at breakfast and put our thoughts together."

"Not using an exquisite place like that makes me uncomfortable," she murmured, looking back at the garden. Maybe she could get out there and walk around before their "instructor" arrived.

"What?"

She gave him a half smile. "Nothing. I'll be down for breakfast in a few minutes." He needed to leave before she could shower.

"Okay." He picked up his coffee cup and

paused in the open door. "Do you want to sleep in here or my room tonight?"

She choked on the hot brew and coughed violently as it burned her windpipe. Her eyes watered as she met his concerned expression. "Why the hell would I sleep in your room?"

"My staff will be here in the morning. Theresa arrives at 6 a.m. She'll definitely notice if we're not sleeping together." The sanguine delivery did not ease the shock of his statement.

"We have a no-sex clause. Are you forgetting that?"

Amusement settled across his face and he leaned on the doorjamb. "Hence the use of the word 'sleep.' The beds are more than large enough for us to share and not touch. But she'll notice and remember. You agreed to perform twenty-four, seven. Theresa only comes on Tuesdays, Wednesdays and Fridays. I gave her a couple of days off to get you settled, but she's here tomorrow. Those nights, we have to sleep together. The rest of the week you can sleep in here."

He was serious.

"Why can't we just get up and slip into the other room via the deck upstairs?" It seemed a little clandestine to plot "waking up" together, but that would be preferable to actually sharing a bed.

"She's going to come in and clean your room. It's part of her job. She'll notice the bed's been slept in. Don't worry, Alyx." The slow grin spreading across his lips had a decidedly unsettling effect on her equilibrium. "I won't bite. See you downstairs in ten. We have a lot to do."

"Thirty," she called after him belatedly, but the door already shut. She stared at her rumpled bed. She could sleep in the car on those nights or...

Her shoulders relaxed. Okay, she could sleep on the floor in his room or the sofa. If his room was anything like hers, it would have plenty of space. Her heart knocked against her ribs and she drained the coffee. If he kept dropping these surprises on her, she would need to add some vodka to the coffee to keep up.

Shower first.

Round two would arrive as soon as she went downstairs.

~

DANIEL

Daniel checked his list for the third time and glanced at his watch. She'd lingered in the shower far past the ten minutes he'd instructed. On the one hand, he liked that she enjoyed the house, more because she didn't have to sleep in her car. On the other, he had two back-to-back video conferences and he wanted to go over the list before they started.

Breakfast on Theresa's off days was fruit, fresh croissants delivered from a local bakery and coffee. He drank his third cup and switched the tablet's screen over to his schedule. He would have to talk to Lucy about rearranging the next few days. The Tokyo meetings couldn't be put off, but most of those were scheduled for three and four in the morning.

The squeak of tennis shoes sliding on tile floor announced the arrival of the prospective princess. "Remember to skip the hop down the stairs tomorrow morning." He didn't glance up in case she saw amusement in his face. Her first morning, she'd slid down the banister. Straddled it *and* slid down. He'd stood in the shadow of the living room, certain she'd seen him, but when she hesitated and looked around before throwing her leg over and riding the rail down, he'd realized she hadn't.

For just a moment, her expression had turned radiant and open. He saw the laughter in her smile and pure joy in the sparkle of her eyes. It took his breath away. He should have chastised her, but he didn't want to erase that whimsical moment.

Not for anything.

"I know." She drew out the words dramatically and tiptoed over to the table. "I will be light as a feather. You won't know I'm here."

"I doubt that." He always knew when she was in the room, whether she sat and drank her coffee quietly or flipped through the paper with the speed of a child searching for the comics. She filled every room with her sheer presence. Even if his P.I. hadn't tracked down her birth certificate and traced her parents, he would have known she was something special.

"Don't worry. I do actually know how to walk. I'm just tired and not particularly looking forward to having my every move watched." She sat in the chair to his right, one bare leg crossing over the other. Despite two shopping trips, she still wore her own clothes.

"And don't look at me like that. There's no staff here and this Victor person knows what we are—I'm not on display." She munched on a croissant and reached over to snatch the paper, pulling out the trade section.

He put a finger on the corner. "List first. Paper second."

"Yes, sir. Right away, sir." She wiped her fingers on a napkin and accepted the digital tablet. He scrolled it back to the list and waited as she read. She pulled one leg onto the chair, her sneakered foot resting on the fabric and her chin on her knee, toes tapping.

She never quite sat still. A multitude of expressions washed over her face as she read. They traveled like lightning, or Santa Ana wind propelled clouds. Curiosity, surprise, irritation, amusement—every new emotion chased away the first. "You're worried about eating in public with me? Do I chew with my mouth open or something?"

"No." He nodded to her leg. "But Victor wanted a very specific list of what might make us uncomfortable. You don't seem to mind how you sit on furniture."

Her foot hit the floor with a thump and she

gave him a long, hard stare. "Would you like me to pretend that we have company now?"

"It wouldn't hurt." He found her quirks charming, but they wouldn't win them points with the press. Not with a long line of royal darlings like the Princesses Grace, Caroline, Diana and Kate. If not for the charade they had to perform, he wouldn't mind.

Alyx shifted in the seat, her posture straightened and she crossed one leg over the other. Her chin came up, coolness breezed over her eyes and her eyebrow lifted. Despite the tank top, shorts and ponytail, she radiated elegance. "Happy?"

"Incredibly." He leaned back in the chair and steepled his fingertips together. She took his breath away, fresh scrubbed without any trace of cosmetics. He could stare at her all day just to see the next bluster of emotion blow through, but the clock ticked and they had work to do. The EU contract bids would begin accepting proposals within six months according to all his sources. Once he had a launching pad into that market, he could afford to indulge other whims.

He forced himself to focus and tapped the digital tablet. "What makes you uncomfortable?"

CHAPTER 6
ALYX

Victor Russell was not what she expected. He stood just over six feet in height, and his ice-blue eyes coupled with his stern expression showed little emotion. Steel-gray hair crowned his head and he wore an impeccable suit. He'd taken a seat in the wing-back chair occupied by Martin during their last meeting after she shook his hand. Daniel sat to his left while she, once again, sat alone on the sofa. She leaned forward, hands clasped and elbows on her knees.

For some reason, the flutters in her stomach increased every moment the man remained silent. She knew him by reputation only—star maker, mover and a shaker. He didn't work on movies, scripts or television. He worked on the actors. He was the premiere acting coach on the West Coast, in high demand on the East, liked to pick and choose his clients, and that exclusive list was not for public consumption, either.

Closing a cover on his digital tablet, the man

caught her staring. He lifted his chin and studied her. Sitting up straighter, she pushed her shoulders back. "Mr. Voldakov, what you're asking for is going to take an inordinate amount of time and attention to detail." Each clearly enunciated word pronounced judgment. Skepticism ran rampant in his tone. "Miss Dagmar, here, has potential, but this is not just a role she can put on and shed. Nor, for that matter, can you. You will have to inhabit it, live and breathe it, day in and day out."

"We are aware of that." Daniel met his steel-laced doubt with a calmness she envied. "We're also one hundred percent on board. Aren't we, Alyx?"

"Absolutely." But her smile faltered as Mr. Russell turned those laser-beam eyes on her.

"Alyx? Not darling or sweetheart? Or some other drippy pet name?" He transferred the hard look back to Daniel. "*You're* sitting over there. *She's* on the sofa. She has her hands clasped so hard together her knuckles are white. Yours are gripping the chair and you've got a pinched look to your smile. A physical gulf between you is interpreted as emotional distance. If you want to sell this, you have to be comfortable touching and being close."

Her stomach cramped and she sat straighter as Daniel rose and moved toward the sofa. He sat next to her, the soft fabric of his pants leg brushing against her bare thigh. Her skin crackled like the release of static electricity, but without the sting.

"Better, but Miss Dagmar shifted to the left a

little. She didn't turn to watch you nor did she smile."

She wanted to embrace this activity—it was a learning experience—but impatience crawled through her at the judgment in his tone. "We're just getting started on this—"

"No, you've been dating for months, secretly indulging in an affair that presumably has left you crazy for each other. You should crave his nearness, enjoy his touch and reciprocate. When he leans in, so should you. When he touches you, you should touch him. Romance is more that soft kisses and headlines. It's body language. Neither of you have the right body language." He tapped a finger against the folder.

"Are you interested in this challenge, Mr. Russell?" Daniel traced a finger down her thigh and she didn't dare move, although just the brush of his knuckles left tingles in its wake. It took every ounce of willpower to not bolt. The "no sex" rule, however, couldn't apply in public. They had to look like they'd had sex.

Lots of it.

How else would they appear comfortable together?

"I think I would enjoy it. I have the standard nondisclosure agreements for all of us, and your attorney has mine on file. It looks like we'll be spending a lot of time together, you should clear your schedule, Mr. Voldakov. Miss Dagmar, why don't you take his hand while we talk? You need to get used to being able to touch each other casually without reacting negatively to the contact."

The weight of two stares bore down on her. One of her acting classes relied heavily on breathing technique. Controlled respiration allowed an actor to handle uncomfortable moments without looking uncomfortable. Her instructor'd reminded them frequently that roles demanded intimacy, the ability to kiss, touch and sell a relationship that didn't necessarily exist anywhere but the screen.

I can do this. She forced her fingers to unlock from each other and dropped her right hand to cover his. His knuckles rubbed her leg as he turned his hand over, catching her palm to palm. Electricity sizzled through her.

Breathe in through the nose and out through the mouth.

Reciting that mantra over and over, she gave Russell a triumphant look. A smile barely curled his lips.

"Starting today, whenever the two of you are together, you need to be touching. Hand on a shoulder, arms around each other, hand in hand —whatever it takes. Constant contact will increase the natural flow of it." He flipped the cover of the tablet open. "Let's say we'll meet each morning at ten? Review how the two of you are doing. Afternoons, I'll spend with Miss Dagmar. I'll bring in a personal shopper and we can expand her wardrobe. We'll also need a consultation on cosmetics, a jeweler... Do you have a ring for her?"

Daniel released her hand and stood. He produced a slender platinum band with a teardrop-shaped diamond. He reached for her hand and her fingers trembled. He slid it slowly onto the third finger of her left hand. She watched the band glide over her knuckle. A shiver of apprehension zinged through her and she couldn't help holding her hand up to examine at the ring.

Despite everything she'd said about not being interested in the jewelry, possessiveness swarmed up at the solitaire twinkling in the morning light. "It's beautiful." The word rode out on a sigh.

"Perfect." Russell applauded and jolted her back to the sitting room—the acting coach, and the billionaire paying her to be his fiancée.

Her hand dropped back to her leg and Daniel reclaimed the other one, but the warmth flooding through her veins cooled. The diamond was a beautiful prop. An exquisitely beautiful prop and she'd fallen for it. "What's next?"

LESS THAN AN HOUR after Russell arrived, Daniel abandoned her to take some phone calls. She watched him leave with more than a little apprehension. Russell'd interrogated them, going over how they met, where their first date had been, correcting them whenever they fumbled or didn't deliver the line with the right amount of emotion.

"Is he a good lover?" Russell asked, the bald

bluntness of the question smashing her distraction.

"I'm sorry?" She glared at him—lesson or not, that was hardly an appropriate question.

"I like it." He tipped his head critically. "A little too much outrage, because those questions will come up. But the imperious note fits the situation."

"You really think that someone is going to ask me if Daniel is a good lover?"

Is he?

"Absolutely, someone from the press is bound to ask you inappropriate questions. It's the nature of the game. Let's take a break from this, however, and work on your walk." He rose and she followed him, grateful for the reprieve. He tucked the folder into his briefcase. "I'll wait while you change."

"What's wrong with this?" Granted, her clothing wasn't elegant, but she needed some modicum of comfort.

"You look like a teenager heading to the Santa Monica pier to cruise for boys, not a princess receiving morning visitors."

"Okay, I get the touching thing, the sitting up thing, the ring thing. But no one can see us, so why do I need to dress up?"

"Not an unfair question." He rebuttoned his suit jacket and faced her. "A princess, however, has no off time. She is always to be presented at her absolute best. You must act as though you are always on display, because when word leaks that a very real princess lives here, you will be. The staff will watch you, the press will watch you and Daniel will watch you. That type of scrutiny is a burden and your manners, your appearance and your attitude must all become second nature or you risk slipping at the wrong moment."

Russell made a fair point. This was the type of method acting she'd craved, but *all* the time?

"Okay." It would take some mental as well as physical adjustment. The agreement was that she live the part, but she'd naturally presumed behind closed doors she would have a break. "You're right. I'm sorry."

Russell continued to watch her, his expression far from unkind. "It's a difficult role you've decided to tackle. One that you are going to have to let consume you...if you want to become the Princess Alyxandretta."

"I can't be Alyx anymore?" At all? Weren't they dressing her up to be herself?

"Likely not. It would be too easy to forget, to get tired, and then you drop the charade."

She didn't imagine the sympathy in his voice. Her life didn't belong to her anymore and wouldn't for the next few months. She'd voluntarily signed it over to Daniel Voldakov's crazy plan. *Eye on the prize. Great acting experience, name recognition, career gold.*

"Okay, I'll change. Will you meet me in the garden?" She turned, searching the doorways beyond the main hall that connected the living room to the rest of the house. "I think it's over there."

"I have some phone calls to make, take your

time. A morning suit would be appropriate. A blouse, a jacket, a skirt and low heels. It's summer, choose something with color—green or peach, perhaps. Both would flatter you."

She didn't receive clothing advice from a man twice her age that often, or ever actually. "Okay. Thirty minutes?"

"It would be my honor, Your Imperial Highness."

Oh, yeah. *That* would take some getting used to. Russell's smile told her he knew it, which meant he'd likely call her that more often. "Okay, thank you." Did she curtsy or was that something royalty received and didn't deliver? Uncertain, she left it alone and escaped up the stairs.

I wanted to take an immersion class...
But this isn't immersion, is it?

Two hours later, her eagerness faded like a worn-out puppy in a play park. She wanted to strangle Russell. Her feet protested the uncomfortable pair of creamy heels that she rarely wore because they were the only shoes that matched her cream-colored suit. She didn't have a green one. The pale pink blouse beneath it added a touch of color, but Russell clucked at it when she arrived at the garden. This outfit was more suited to a wedding than a morning walk, which was why she'd purchased it in the first place.

They walked in a slow circuit. The too-casual slow pace made her crazy.

"Your Imperial Highness, fidgeting is a sign of boredom. At no point when you are meeting with others or presenting in public can you allow yourself to look bored. Calm, serene, engaged. These are the three words you want to remember." He caught everything. If she rolled her eyes, twisted her fingers or, heaven help her, tapped her foot.

"We've been at this for hours, Mr. Russell. I need a break." Her shoulders slumped. Just a few hours into the charade and she wanted out. What the heck did that say about her future career choices?

"Quitting, Your Imperial Highness?" The challenge tweaked her pride.

Her chin came up. "No. But I wish to sit, to eat and to have a respite from the lesson."

"Very well." He glanced at his watch. "It's just now one. Let's reconvene at two-thirty."

"You're not joining us for lunch?" Daniel chose that moment to appear. He caught her left hand and lifted it, brushing one kiss to the finger bearing his ring. The action kick-started her sluggish system.

"Very nicely done, Mr. Voldakov. Her Imperial Highness still needs some work. But I have a rule —I do not sit at a table with clients unless it is part of the lesson, and the princess has requested a break."

Guilt stabbed at her. The man shouldn't miss a meal because she'd whined.

"I ordered in the food. It arrived about twenty minutes ago. If you want to eat in the solarium, we'll take the dining room." Daniel didn't appear to share her hesitation. He tucked her arm into his.

"Thank you." Russell nodded to both of them, adding a bit of a bow to her. "I'll see you at two-thirty, promptly, Princess. We'll take the discussion inside. I think we can spend some time on language, history and etiquette this afternoon."

"Yay," she murmured, but he was already out of earshot.

Daniel ducked his head down to catch her gaze. "Tired?"

"Exhausted. The man can walk." She wanted to peel off her shoes and walk barefoot across the cool tiles inside the house. So tired, she didn't object to Daniel leading her to the dining room. The smell of fresh grilled fish and vegetables elicited a fierce growl from her stomach. Two cups of coffee and a croissant didn't cut it against the stress.

He held her chair and caressed her nape as she sat. She pulled away, but his hand didn't retreat. "We have to get used to this," he reminded her.

"I need a break, okay? Just for this hour— we're not on display. No one here to impress." The disconcerting sensations his every touch elicited didn't help either.

"A small one. It might be easier to pretend touch when you don't have to worry about what people are seeing." He uncovered her plate before sitting down to his own silver-topped dish. Her mouth watered at the food.

For a man used to servants and hired help, he did do an awful lot for himself.

It didn't matter that some tasks only required

picking up a phone to call in an order, he took care of them.

She flipped out the napkin and tossed it over her lap. He touched his calf to hers and another jolt sparked through her. He cut into his fish without looking up and she sighed, covering her discomfort with a swallow of cold water.

"I know you're not having fun, but I think the learning curve will be the worst part." His empathy sounded genuine. "Just remember, we're a team in this."

"Where are your heels, then?"

He laughed and brushed her leg with his in a soothing fashion. "Suits and ties are my heels, Al —sweetheart." He caught himself. "But how about a foot rub when the torture is over tonight? It's the least I can do."

"I may hold you to that." She speared a bite of salmon and sighed at the sweet melted butter and hint of peppers on the flaky fish.

"I hope you will."

Something in his voice tugged her head up and she met his easy smile. For a moment, she forgot about his leg brushing hers or the weight on her finger. It was just lunch with a handsome guy.

"Okay, then. I will." Decided, she concentrated on the food. They had a lot of work to do.

CHAPTER 7
DANIEL

Daniel rubbed the back of his neck as the driveway gates closed behind Victor's departing car. Exhaustion weighed on his shoulders and his head ached. They'd sat through the most grueling dinner in his recent memory. Victor insisted they hold hands, and Daniel took every opportunity to explore her smooth skin, the way her fingers cupped his, and when she'd had to take her hand back to eat, he'd glided a leg against her.

The initial instruction to get used to touching her came a lot easier than he imagined and carried its own particular brand of torture. Locking up and engaging the security system, he found the downstairs lights already dimmed. Alyx'd escaped up the stairs at the first opportunity, almost, but not quite, rolling her eyes when Victor'd announced he would return after breakfast.

His gaze wandered toward the stairs. Because the first month would be the hardest, he told the office he would be working from home. He had two programs to review. Despite having a large staff of developers, he was a hands-on kind of guy. No Spherecast software went into production without his review. But he didn't want to work—they were supposed to share the same room tonight. He could have given her an out by giving Theresa the week off, but the sparkle in Alyx's eyes and the challenge in the stubborn jut of her chin were too attractive to resist.

Upstairs, he paused outside the room he'd given to her and listened. No sound echoed from within. Bypassing her room, he walked to his own door and hesitated. Knocking once, he let her know he planned to enter and twisted the knob at her muffled "come in."

Alyx curled up on the sofa beneath the window that made up the whole exterior wall. He loved the natural light and the profusion of windows in the house attracted him the first time he toured it with a realtor. She'd stolen a pillow from the bed and laid out one blanket against the cushions, and sandwiched herself beneath another one. She was brushing her hair and gave him a wry smile as he stared.

"You said we had to sleep in the same room, but if you sleep in the middle of your bed, it will be rumpled and I can sleep here. Then we toss the blankets on the bed in the morning to add to the mussed-up effect."

Triumph sparkled in her grin and he shook his head, quashing the nibble of disappointment in the pit of his stomach. "That sofa is hardly big enough for you to sleep on."

"Maybe not for you, Sasquatch, but I fit just fine. See?" She stretched out, extending one bare leg from beneath blanket. Her toes didn't quite reach the other end. "It's a lot bigger than my backseat, I assure you."

He grimaced and tried again. "The bed would be more comfortable." Not to mention, he'd rather looked forward to waking up with her...if they got any sleep.

"I'm sure it is, but I'm fine here." She returned to brushing her hair. In the time he'd taken to send Victor off, she'd changed back into the familiar tank top and shorts. Her face, scrubbed free of makeup, shone and her hair gleamed in the low light of the room.

"Well, the offer's open. If you change your mind, feel free to join me." He let her take the victory for now. They had many more nights stretched out in front of them.

Nothing would help them get used to the intimacy of being together and touching as sharing the same bed.

Or being intimate.

He hid a frown as he closed the door and crossed to the bathroom. A cool shower was the best plan. Unfortunately, he'd agreed to that no-sex clause. It was too bad, too. They could definitely pass the time more pleasantly with sex. Stripping, he turned the shower on, then stepped beneath the cool spray. The chill water braced the raw need heating his body. *We just got started, best to table any changes until later.*

The shower cleared his head and eased the

ache in his neck. Dried off and clad only in boxers, he shut off the bathroom light and opened the door to a dim bedroom. Only the low-wattage light next to the bed burned. Alyx slept with her back to him, the blanket outlining her silhouette beautifully.

Clock set for five, he punched the pillows and stretched out under the sheet before shutting the remaining light off. Tucking an arm behind his head, he stared up into the darkness. As tired as he felt, sleep remained elusive. The soft, regular sound of her breathing filtered through the quiet. The sheet was too warm. He pushed it off and rolled onto his side, looking for a comfortable position.

An hour later, tired of staring into the darkness, he gave up. Careful to be quiet, he used his phone as a flashlight and padded toward the door.

"Can't sleep?" Her voice whispered through the blackness.

"Nope. Sorry, didn't mean to wake you. Just going to go downstairs."

"Hang on." The blankets rustled. "I'll come with you."

He pulled the door open to let the low light from the hallway in, but was a little too late as her knee hit the corner of the bed. He winced in sympathy.

"I'm fine." She hopped. "Ow. That smarts."

"Next time we'll just turn on the light." He flipped the wall switch and gave her an apologetic smile.

"S'okay. I'll live. After you." She motioned for him to precede her and they trundled down the stairs. "Why can't you sleep?"

"No idea." He finished the answer with a jaw-popping yawn. "I'm tired."

"Me too. I don't suppose you have any ice cream?" The question surprised him and awakened a mild craving. Ice cream did sound good.

"Let's find out."

In the kitchen, the freezer air was too damn cold on his bare chest, but he pulled out a tub of chocolate chip. "Aha."

"Excellent." She grinned and disappeared into the pantry, returning with chocolate syrup. He set the tub on the counter and went in search of bowls. "Where's the ice-cream scoop?" she asked, opening one drawer after another.

"Two to the right of the dishwasher." Setting the stoneware bowls on the counter, he paused to open the top on the ice-cream container. "I think we've got whipped cream too."

"If you have nuts, I may die of happiness."

"Noted. I won't tell you there are dessert toppings in the cupboard to the right of the fridge." He found the can of spray whip in the fridge and shook it. Alyx skipped over and pulled the cupboard open. He leaned past her, shoulders brushing, to grab the nuts. "See, no nuts."

She laughed and pressed a hand to his chest as she hopped to try and snag the plastic bag, but he swept it away, grinning. She pursued him and grabbed the ice-cream scoop. "Surrender the nuts or I'll keep the ice cream to myself."

"Ha, you play mean." He squinted at her. "How about I give you the nuts and you give me the scoop?"

"At the same time?" Her brows rose. "Hmm... Can I trust you?"

"To give you some nuts? Why not?" The corner of his mouth curled upward.

"Because you're sneaky." She eyed the bag, a look of longing softening her face. "Okay, at the same time. We both put them down."

"Right. On three."

"One." She grinned and stretched the scoop toward the counter.

"Two." He lowered the nuts.

"Three." She darted forward and snaked the bag right out of his hand, but he caught her on the escape, one arm banding around her middle and dragging her back against him. She squealed with laughter and he took advantage of her full hands to tickle her sides.

"That's cheating," he warned her and she squirmed, trying to evade his hands, and only managed to rub against him. His cock roused, half stiffening, and he grabbed the scoop *and* nuts before forcing himself to release her.

She danced away, eyes sparkling and her hands covering her bright smile. "Sorry, I couldn't resist."

Yeah, neither can I.

"You first," he offered graciously, sweeping an arm toward the counter and retreating behind it so she couldn't see the wood tenting his shorts.

No sex. No sex. No sex. If you break the damn contract, she's out and then we're screwed.

Martin thought his drive to make this deal—to pursue this contract with Alyx and use her royal connection—was about pride, and partially it was—but if Spherecast didn't grow, if it didn't stay at the forefront and ahead of his competitors, then his bigger contracts might switch out and the whole house of cards tumbled.

"Such a gentleman."

If she only knew, but he contented himself watching her scoop two generous balls of ice cream into her bowl and grinned when she added some to his as well.

"I warn you, I make a terrific sundae. I used to work at an ice-cream shop in high school. We had to make every single dessert on the menu—and they had *a lot*—to be sure we got the presentation right." She drizzled chocolate in perfect swirls on both before claiming the whipped cream and adding a generous mound. The nuts she sprinkled with care, and slipped a spoon into the side of his bowl before passing it over. "Sugar's up."

"Looks good." He put a spoonful of the confection in his mouth. The sugar overload hit like a brick, but she was right—it was spectacular.

"Thank you." She dug right into hers, and they ate in relative quiet on opposite sides of the kitchen island. "What kind of software do you create?"

"Hmm?" He lifted a brow, chasing an escapee nut trying to sink into the melting ice cream.

"Spherecast? It's a software company. What kind of software do you do? I mean—video games? Finance software? Shoe comparison app that lets you take a picture of shoes and finds them for you online?" A drip of chocolate hovered at the corner of her mouth. It looked more edible than the ice-cream sundaes.

"We design a lot of things." And he needed to stop staring at her mouth. "Water?"

"Actually, I want coffee. I know it's weird, but I always get cold after eating ice cream—which is the point, I know. But coffee sounds good. Maybe? Please?" She batted her eyelashes in such a patently false show of modesty that he laughed.

"Sure. Have a preference?" He motioned to the espresso machine then the single cup maker. The single-cup maker also had a carafe option. He preferred straight black coffee when he was working. At her shrug, he just flicked the carafe option on. He could reset it when they were done.

"Define a 'lot of things'?" She licked her spoon clean and claimed both their bowls to rinse out in the sink.

"Finance software." He waited for her nose to wrinkle and suppressed another smile when it did. "Database tools. Retail processing software, shopping carts and occasionally a video game here or there. We're just getting our feet wet in that department, though. Mostly we specialize in high-end security, network internal and external." He picked up the ice-cream tub and the whipped-cream can to put them back where they went. In a couple of minutes the center island was clean and she wiped it with a damp cloth as the carafe burbled and hissed the last of the brew.

"Huh. Why software? I mean I know it's lucrative, but why did you get into designing it?" She rinsed her hands off and passed him the two coffee cups they drank out of and washed up that morning.

Filling both, he shrugged. "Just something I was good at. I got my first computer when I was eight or nine. Wrote my first program at ten and never looked back."

"What was your first program?" She sipped the coffee and leaned back against the counter, looking more relaxed than she had all day.

"You'll laugh." His lips twisted and he took a drink of the coffee. She was right—it was the perfect level of heat to chase away the chill of their dessert.

"I promise, I'll try not to laugh too hard." Her impudent, irrepressible grin drew him. He liked her brand of honesty.

"It was a stats tool."

She squinted one eye closed and tilted her head. "How would that be funny?"

"Because," he lifted his mug, "it was for an online game so I could get the best gear with the most attributes for my characters."

Her mouth opened. "Why?"

"Because a lot of the good gear was BOP." At her quizzical look, he chuckled. He'd already let his inner nerd out of the bag. "It means bind on pickup. When you went on raids with groups, you had to know whether you could really use an item before you took it, because you couldn't give it away. Raids were a big thing and you were often limited to winning one item. I wanted to make sure whatever item I was after I could use and was the best for my character class. I created a database that let me see how adding or taking away a piece would affect my overall strength, health and talents. The best combos I saved and that way I knew what to get."

"What you're saying is that it was a shoe comparison program for geeks?" No malice or criticism echoed in her words, but the analogy wasn't that far off.

"More or less."

She grunted, the corners of her eyes crinkling. "That's kind of cool."

"Yeah, well, I thought so. When it worked well, I put it on the net—that way others could use it—and in six months I had a lot of hits and an offer from the game company to buy it. They wanted to add it to their own tools on their site."

"All right. It's funny, but I'm impressed. How old were you?"

"Eleven—or twelve maybe. I'd really tweaked the software by then, and set it up so all I had to do was update it with new tables for new equipment during game updates. But after I sold it to them, they charged a subscription fee to use it. That kind of annoyed me, because the work was done and the players already paid to play the game. But I learned from that error in judgment. The next time I built something like that I made it free, and I didn't take a gaming company's offer to buy it out." It also gave him the drive to look into computer degrees and programming design in high school. By his senior year, he'd finished three college-level courses and had gotten a full scholarship to CalTech.

"That's really cool."

"What about you? Why acting?" He regretted the question the moment he asked it. The cheerful gleam in her eyes shuttered behind a more guarded expression. She retreated from the easy intimacy of the chat and he was left to wonder why.

"That's a long story for another night." She finished the cup and rinsed it out, setting it on the counter. "I think I'll try to get some sleep now."

He wanted to pursue the issue, but she walked away and the stiffness returned to her posture. "I think I'll do some work. Be up in a bit."

"Night," she called back.

Blowing out a long breath he looked down at his still-semi erect cock pressing against the front of his shorts. He definitely needed to focus on software for a bit or he would never get any sleep. Alyx was an employee—he needed to keep that straight in his head. Yes, he didn't want her sleeping in her car, but he'd hired her for a specific task. It helped no one to let lust override his judgment.

CHAPTER 8
ALYX

Alyx trailed her fingers down the length of fabric. The pure silk glided against her skin in sensuous invitation, but one look at the price tag and she moved on to the next dress on the rack. Victor cut in front of her and pointed to the dress. "What's wrong with that one?"

His six-foot-two-inch frame was more than a roadblock and she sighed. "Nothing's wrong with it, exactly, but it's not what I'm looking for."

"Hmm. And what are you looking for? We need at least four cocktail dresses, two evening gowns, a dozen daytime suits and changes. Specifically, you need a change of clothes for each meal." He consulted the data tablet he carried everywhere. "Then there will be the shoes."

Lips pursed, she swallowed back laughter. In his button-down steel-gray suit and thousand-dollar shoes, he looked more suited to an executive office—his tense expression said "secret service, stay away." He constantly seemed to scan their surroundings, aware of everything. Often enough for her to notice. The behavior disconcerted her, but his persistence in encouraging her to shop was too funny.

"They're expensive." She lowered her voice, keeping her expression calm and the intonation smooth. Two people could have a knock-down-drag-out verbal match and no one would notice if their voices didn't raise and their tone didn't change. "There's a consignment shop in Santa Barbara that has some spectacular gowns for a twelfth the price—if that." She could feed herself for a month on real meals for the price of the decadently soft silk dress.

Her escort tapped his fingers against the rack. "You don't look at the price tags."

"What?"

"You never look at the price tag. The price is irrelevant. You are shopping for clothing, to costume the platform you will be performing from. Money isn't the issue, nor is the price. You look only at color, fabric and effect." Like her, he never raised his voice, but the hair on her body prickled at the low command. "A princess doesn't shop consignments."

Which is the most ridiculous thing ever. How many articles hit the papers about the expenses of the royal families in Europe? When Prince William and his bride visited the United States, comments were made about the number of outfits Kate was photographed in and the concept of excess versus frugality. Some liked her frugal nature, and others didn't. Rebellion surged through her. The fact she recycled her clothes and popular outfits returned, like normal people, also got noticed. Why spend money like that if one didn't have to? There were better things money could be spent on.

Like feeding people, sending kids to school, paying off bills...

Getting an apartment, which would have saved me this entire adventure because I would have been behind a locked door when Daniel got his crazy idea.

As quickly as the rebellion surfaced, so did the nibble of worry that she may have missed out on meeting the sweet man she'd shared ice cream with the night before. He could be fun and funny. A thrill skated over her skin. The tickling antics delighted her, more than she wanted to admit.

Victor flicked through the rack, then pulled out a dress and held it up to her. The deep blue sheath boasted an off-one-shoulder neckline and tucked fabric that would accent her curves and smooth any flaws in her figure. It fell to just above her knees. "How about we choose a selection, you try them on and if you can't find fault with how you look, we take it?" he coaxed with his voice and gentle expression.

"Fine." She nodded. "Do you want to just pick out the dresses and I'll go start trying them on?"

Disapproval creased his forehead and he sighed.

"Or I could just take a good look at what they have?"

He nodded and she resisted the urge to rub a hand over her face. Fidgeting in public got her chastised once, she wouldn't do it again. Together, they strolled through the racks, picking out a dozen different dresses. At the dressing rooms, Victor requested the private one off to the side with a stern glance at the clerk. This flustered the young woman attending, but she hurried to help them.

"You know, we have several shoes that would go great with those dresses." The salesclerk cut her gaze down to Alyx's feet. "You're a six, yes?"

At her slow nod, the clerk beamed. "I'll be right back. Just take your time." She hustled off and Victor leaned against the wall, taking a position between the changing room and the rest of the store.

"I guess we're getting shoes too."

"Apparently." He nodded approvingly and flicked his gaze to the changing room. Accepting the subtle nudge, she stepped inside and surveyed the dresses. She'd worn a simple, slimming pair of slacks and a blousy top for shopping. Both sported designer labels and both were purchased at the consignment shop he'd just dismissed for less than three dollars each. Amused, she stuck out her tongue at the closed door.

The crushed linen held up well with constant changes and didn't wrinkle in the car. The pale peach color emphasized her tan and accented the green chemise she wore beneath as well as the dyed-to-match green flats.

If only Victor knew she'd dyed the shoes herself. She'd actually found them at an off-the-rack wedding shop. But she thought that a secret best kept to herself. Hanging her outfit up on the empty hangers, she studied the dresses. She'd worn a bra, but at least two of them would require a strapless variety and she planned to try those on last. Reorganizing the dresses, she started—left to right.

The first, a yellow and orange sunrise of a dress, wasn't particularly a cocktail outfit but she needed daytime event dresses as well. The color was a risk, but the shades were beautiful and she wanted to see if it would work. The neckline plunged between her breasts, but the halter top emphasized her shape. The handkerchief skirt swirled around her legs and she did a little hop-twirl and laughed.

"Find something you like?" Victor's voice drifted over the stall door, reminding her she wasn't alone.

Pulling her hair up into a mock ponytail, she swung the door inward and glided out on light feet. The dress did wonders to improve her mood. She caught sight of herself in the far mirrors and turned—it also shaped her ass nicely, smoothing over the curve, and accented her figure without being overly revealing.

"Cocktail parties at the beach. Afternoon tea." Victor canted his head critically. "A polo match, were you to attend one."

The clerk's soft gasp turned Alyx all the way around and she let go of her hair.

"You look amazing in that. I have a couple of

necklaces that you should try. Tourmaline. I'll just call down to the jewelry counter and have those sent straight up." She balanced several boxes of shoes. Victor shifted to the side, but rather than offer to take them, he merely made room for her.

"You could help her." Alyx went for sotto voce, but the clerk laughed, her pixie cut bouncing as she set the boxes down and knelt.

"Private security doesn't usually want their hands filled with boxes, ma'am." A furtive look crossed her expression. "And don't worry, we're absolutely discreet here. Now, I have these in a six, but I think our wedge sandals would really set that dress off, but I only have that in a six and a half. We'll try those and if you like them, I can get them ordered and delivered to you within twenty-four hours. Less, if you need them today."

Alyx would have corrected her, but one glimpse of Victor's satisfied expression and she held her tongue. "Thank you."

She tolerated the woman helping her into the shoes. The six and a halfs were definitely too big, but the moment she saw the effect of the wedge heels on her legs in the mirror, she knew she had to have them. Her calves stretched and shaped beautifully. The orange and yellow mixture in the shoes was a perfect complement to the dress.

The clerk wrote the shoe's identification number and size down. "Would you like one or two pairs? We actually have these in a sand color that would complement the earth-tone version of this dress."

Why order one pair when two would do and a second dress could be sold? Victor tapped two fingers against his wrist.

"Two please." Alyx smiled. "The sand and the yellow. They're beautiful. Thank you."

"Absolutely. I'll go get that dress for you—seven, yes?"

The woman had an impeccable eye. Alyx nodded and tried not to swallow her tongue at the price tag on the shoes. She gave Victor a bland look and glided back in to change. She had a care with the dress and the shoes. Next up was a calf-length sheath in all black with a ribbed bodice that snugged against her so tightly she didn't think she'd be able to breathe.

Christine, the clerk, returned in the time it took Alyx to shimmy into the black body wrap that doubled as a dress. Alyx could breathe, but only just barely. Thank God the skirt boasted a slit behind her knees or she'd never have been able to walk. A brief smile of approval lit up Victor's dour expression. Christine braced a pair of elegant stilettos and Alyx stepped into one, then the other.

The effect was dramatic. She gained four inches of height and added a voluptuous curve to her lean build. This dress emphasized her less than stellar boobs and her ass no longer looked like it needed a lift.

"You need one in every color like this." Christine made more notes. "I've got shoes to go with each shade, but I think the green would be best and of course, you can never go wrong in black.

For this one, a nice diamond set for your neck and ears, a tennis bracelet to give it that look of simple purity."

Christine fussed over her, turning her around and checking the fit. "Hair up, too. It is a bit on the snug side, but it's supposed to be... We could let it out a quarter of an inch, but I hate to destroy the way this accentuates your build." She turned Alyx around to look at the mirror. With swift pins she fastened the russet hair up into a twist of curls on top of her head, tendrils escaping to wisp along her cheeks.

"Innocent. Serene. Perfect."

Alyx didn't recognize the woman in the mirror—with her chin up and the dress and hair, she saw an elegant stranger. Her eyes burned and she blinked to force the tears back.

"Did I say something wrong?" Christine's hopeful expression fell.

"Not at all." She patted the woman soothingly on the arm. "It's just very lovely, and it took me by surprise how much. I'd like three, please. One in purple as well, rather than red, if you have it."

"I absolutely can get it for you in purple, Your—ma'am." The clerk cleared her throat and helped her out of the shoes, unzipping the dress before opening the changing room door, and Alyx slipped inside. As the door closed, she flattened her hand against the wall. Christine seemed to be in on the secret. The near slip revealed a lot and she sucked in a deep breath, forcing the panic to subside. She ended up with a dozen more dresses to try on. But for some reason, this didn't feel like acting anymore. It was real.

I can do this...

~

DANIEL

"He's still not returning our calls. I spoke to Prentiss and he's assured me that the grand duke will be in touch as soon as he returns from his Mediterranean jaunt." Martin dropped a file onto the desk with a grunt of frustration.

"Take it easy, old man. We'll be fine." He patted the lawyer on the shoulder. It didn't matter that he shared Martin's anxiety, maybe more. But if Andraste was out of the country, then maybe he wasn't meeting with potential competitors. That gave Daniel more time and he didn't feel the need to rush. "We don't want him getting back too soon, anyway. We need the time to finish prepping Alyx. Coffee?"

"Sure." The man dropped into a chair and leaned back, one ankle resting on the opposite knee. "How is the princess project going?"

"About ten thousand at Cartier and another fifteen at La Jeune." The calls from the credit company came in fifteen minutes before and Daniel authorized both expenditures. Alyx'd left the house before he woke and the only sign that she'd been there was the rumpled pillow and blanket she'd left on the bed. Theresa told him that Victor picked her up in a limousine and they'd left to shop. His inquisitive housekeeper had obviously wanted to ask more questions, but he let her wonder.

That was Victor's key piece of advice in all this. The fewer people in the know, the fewer who could reveal the truth, but the secret should be advertised. If his staff speculated, the news would begin to filter out. That could only help them. The Spherecast PR department had already received very specific instructions on how they were to "answer" questions and that sparked another flurry of rumors.

He passed Martin the mug of coffee and circled around to sit behind the desk. He didn't dwell on the disappointment he'd experienced at Alyx's absence over breakfast. He'd actually been able to finish his newspaper without someone stealing pages away before he could read them.

"I told you it was going to cost more than you thought. Be careful she doesn't bleed you dry on these little shopping trips." Martin's doubt-laden grimace reminded Daniel that his attorney still didn't approve of the plan.

"It's not her credit card. I authorized Victor Russell on one of the accounts. He's handling the shopping. She hasn't asked for anything really. Except—hang on a sec." He picked up the phone and dialed the number to his house. Theresa answered on the first ring. "Theresa, when is the next grocery trip scheduled?"

"Today, Mr. Voldakov. It's always on Fridays," she reminded him patiently.

"Excellent. Add some chocolate chocolate-chip ice cream, fresh whipped cream, some fruit and more chocolate syrup—and nuts. I think we were nearly out."

"Anything else?"

Daniel drummed his fingers on the desk. "Steaks. Oat milk. And an assortment of flavored creamers..." The few things he did know about his bride-to-be was that she liked red meat and she liked her desserts. She also liked coffee with her dessert and she never touched the half-and-half. He'd seen the glimmers of disappointment after one morning coffee run to the kitchen when she glanced in the refrigerator. She'd avoided espresso since she moved in, but he only had regular milk.

"All right." Theresa cleared her throat. "Do you need any other supplies?"

Daniel blinked slowly. The uncomfortable note in her voice suggested a different issue, but he wasn't quite sure what. "No, I think that's it. Thank you."

"You're very welcome, Mr. Voldakov."

"Huh." Daniel hung up the phone and scratched his jaw.

"Planning to gorge yourself on sugar when this doesn't work out?" Martin's mouth twisted into a sardonic smile.

"No, Alyx likes ice-cream sundaes in the middle of the night. I want to make sure we have plenty. Theresa just sounded odd when she asked if I needed any other supplies." Steak and ice cream were hardly supplies.

"She probably wants to know if you need condoms, but is too polite to ask directly."

He inhaled coffee and set the mug down, coughing and sputtering. Martin couldn't have shocked him more if he'd sucker punched him across the desk. "I don't think I've ever asked her to buy me condoms."

"Two years ago with that model from Nice. You were holed up with her for a week, working on that design-a-babe project." Martin flipped open his laptop.

"It was a pseudo-morphing program for women who were working out to help them identify trouble areas and what exercises would help them achieve success in specific areas of their bodies." *Design-a-babe.* Daniel snorted. *What the hell was that model's name?*

"Po-tay-to, po-tah-to. You called Theresa at home, asked her to deliver some groceries—including condoms—and to take the rest of the week off."

"Because what's-her-name was naked while I did my scans." Daniel straightened in the chair. "The condoms were a precaution." He ignored Martin's dry look. "What's on the agenda today?"

For some reason talking about the model made him uncomfortable, particularly because he hadn't set out to have an affair with the Nordic blonde bombshell, just work with her. But staring at her voluptuous breasts day after day had its effect. Not his proudest moment, but definitely in the past.

"The scholarship project is moving forward.

We received grant status approval and I filed the tax-exemption and that's just a waiting game. But I imagine by the first of next month we'll be able to announce the fund—*Spherecast Technologies Scholarship*. It has a good ring to it."

"No, it should be the Dagmar Fund for Further Education or the Princess Alyxandretta Charity—don't put our name on it." It was Alyx's idea. She should get the credit. "We can hold that announcement in our pocket for an event and use it to launch her as well."

"If you say so." Martin's tone indicated severe doubt.

"Spit it out before you choke on it." Daniel sat forward. He and Martin had been friends long before he needed his legal advice. One of the few friendships he could attribute to his gaming days that translated better in real life. It was why they worked well together. The man wasn't known for withholding his judgment and Daniel didn't want him to start now.

"You're trusting your company's fiscal future to a waitress from Sonoma. If you had a board of directors they'd string you up." Martin clenched his fingers around his coffee mug. "All you have is her word and a signature on some paperwork that says she won't tank this for you. You're taking one hell of a risk."

"It's my company. It's my risk." He forced himself to maintain a calm tone. Martin had his best interests at heart for one and he'd asked, for two. "She's not going to screw me over. She is doing her best and putting a hell of a lot of effort into a charade she didn't have to bother with."

"You're paying her a million dollars."

"And I offered her five." Daniel thumped the desk. "She could have had a blank check and she didn't ask for it. She doesn't want these clothes, she doesn't want to be a princess, but she's doing it because she accepted the job."

"You don't *know* her. Dammit, Daniel. You're a dreamer, I get that. You dream big ideas and you make them happen. But those are bits and bytes of code on a computer. You can't program this woman to be what you want her to be."

"I don't want to program her to do anything. It's not about what I want, but what I need. She can do this, because she is simply becoming the person she always was." And she didn't sleep in her damn car anymore. "Let this shit go, Martin. Get on board or get out. You think I don't know her? I've been living with her for the past week. She's more comfortable in bare feet than shoes. She prefers pizza to haute cuisine. She actually knows the lyrics to every Madonna song ever recorded, including three I've never heard of. She likes to read, and she has a stuffed bear with a missing eye that she keeps in that beat-up Volvo rather than bring in the house because she's not certain she belongs. I know a hell of a lot about her—leave her alone. Do we understand each other?"

He met his attorney's gaze with a hard look. Whether the "damn fool" idea worked or not, his friend wasn't going to harass Alyx. Not when she was working her ass off to accomplish in a few short weeks what it took most a lifetime to prepare for and it was only going to get worse.

"You're falling for her." Martin exhaled.

"Don't be stupid." Daniel retreated from that line of thinking. "I'm protecting an investment. We've discussed the scholarship, what's next?"

CHAPTER 9
ALYX

A knock on the door announced the housekeeper. Alyx glanced up as Theresa entered. The older woman looked to be in her mid-forties, short dark hair styled away from her face. She didn't wear a uniform, exactly, but she wore a variant on the crisp slacks and polo shirt favored by many of the local spas and health clubs.

"Good morning, Miss Dagmar." Theresa pronounced her last name carefully, but added emphasis to the miss.

"Good morning, Theresa. And, please, call me Alyx." She'd tried three times to get the woman to call her by her given name and three times she'd been politely rebuffed.

It was still early—she'd sneaked out of the bedroom while Daniel still sprawled. Barely six-thirty, almost too early to be up, but she'd rolled over to see her roommate stretched across the bed, sheet riding low over his hips and a morning erection tenting the jersey cotton.

Escape seemed the better part of valor. She'd slipped back to her own room, showered and changed into one of the myriad of morning suits Victor insisted she buy. The coffeemaker brewed in the kitchen and the scent drew her like a moth to a flame. Theresa had offered her a latte with oat milk and that had been a delightful surprise. Cup in hand, she'd settled in the sitting room and rescued the book on the royal families of Europe. Victor and Daniel both said hers was listed in chapter fourteen.

"Thank you, Miss Dagmar. Would you like some more coffee? I'm going to fix breakfast shortly, if you have any preferences." Theresa swept around the room, adjusting the blinds, picking up yesterday's discarded newspaper and emptying trash bins.

Daniel strode into the room on the heels of the statement. "Omelets?" A hopeful note in the request. He turned his devastating smile on her as he circled around Theresa. Alyx's heart pounded as he came right up to the sofa and bent down. His lips brushed hers, lighter than a butterfly or the caress of a feather. His face hovered close to hers as he murmured, "Good morning."

Mouth tingling, she could barely muster a smile with him this close. The scent of his aftershave, a light spice, tickled her nostrils. His blue eyes gleamed as though he possessed a secret and she longed to know how he did that—how he woke up cheerful and happy with the world. "Good morning." The words rode out on a sigh.

"I will make the omelets." Theresa cleared her throat then slipped back out of the room.

Daniel straightened, his gaze following the housekeeper's exit before he glanced back at her. He didn't move away, his warmth like a blanket. He was dressed in his Daniel clothes— business slacks, button-down shirt and loafers—but he'd chosen darker colors today, save for the shirt, which matched his eyes.

"How are you?" He touched her cheek, just a brush really, fingertips gliding over her skin. She could almost forget they weren't involved.

"I'm good." Which, surprisingly enough, she meant. "You?"

He smiled wider and walked over to the coffee service and poured his own cup. "Not bad. I hope I didn't wake you up last night. I had two conference calls with Japan."

"Nope. Didn't hear a thing." That wasn't entirely true. She'd rolled over to see him backlit from the open bathroom door as he got ready to go to bed. The light caressing his muscles and casting his face into shadow filled her dreams for the rest of the night.

Another good reason to escape when he'd looked deliciously relaxed in bed.

"Good." He carried his cup over and lifted her feet, sliding onto the sofa beneath them and tucking her feet against his legs. Thank God she'd chosen slacks rather than one of the skirts. She should move her feet, but he leaned back, his gaze riding up to the windows as he took a sip of coffee.

On closer examination, the faint circles beneath his eyes made him look tired.

Forgetting the book in her lap for the time being, she cradled her coffee cup. "Do you often have meetings that late?"

Surprise crossed his expression. "Unfortunately. Well, not really unfortunate. Two of my client companies lost a lot of information when their data center collapsed. I've been working on a program that helps them rebuild and restore what was lost. But it takes an immeasurable amount of sifting to make it happen—sifting social media postings about their projects, internal message boards, and access to their employees' home computers and laptops."

"I'm not sure what social media would have to do with all of that or why you would be sifting." Frankly, she'd never been a fan of computers. She'd never owned one, nor had she used them outside of the school library. The cheap laptop she'd used for her classes had strictly been for papers or research. By the time she could afford a better one, it'd seemed pointless. She sipped the coffee. Daniel shifted sideways. He still had her feet, but he faced her and stretched one arm out along the back of the sofa.

"Everything you do on a computer is reflected in the machine's active memory. When you add the internet, whether it's a closed intranet or not, it leaves a footprint. Data can be stored in RAM cache—" He paused. "You don't know what that is, do you?"

She shook her head slowly, but he seemed

awfully excited about the "cash" prospects. "Sorry."

"Okay, you remember how with an old camera you could take a picture and you had to develop the negatives first and then you used the negative to get a picture? If you wanted more prints, all you needed was the negative?"

"Yes." Digital cameras and the cameras on phones had replaced those, but she'd actually studied photography for one semester at a high school in Woodland. That was her favorite foster home and best school. Unfortunately, when Pete —her foster father—lost his job, she had to move on. Pushing aside that dismal thought, she focused on Daniel's grin.

"Great. Ram cache is like a negative or snapshot of the information they looked at most recently. If you write the program correctly, it can match parameters—digital edges of one piece of information—with another." He took a swallow of coffee, then set the cup on the table. "Imagine that my right hand is one computer and my left hand is another." He snagged her coffee cup and sat it next to his.

She gave him a gimlet eye, but couldn't suppress a smile at his excitement. "Each of your hands are computers too." He caught her wrists and held her hands up. "Each of our fingers represents a piece of digital data. Let's say that on your right hand computer you were reviewing the company's spreadsheets, available on that intranet, the last page you looked at is your pinkie."

Awareness swarmed up her arm and back down as he wiggled the finger in question. "Your ring and middle fingers were the last two pages of this spreadsheet you reviewed, but your forefinger and thumb are just your login and the book sample you were reading before you got back to work."

She giggled as he wagged a finger at her thumb. "Bad thumb."

Daniel winked. "My left hand is the computer that your coworker was reviewing the same file on. My thumb and forefinger were the pizza we ordered for lunch and the movie tickets I wanted to buy, but my middle finger matches the same sheet your ring finger looked at, while my ring and pinkies are the next two in the sequence before your pinkie." He threaded his fingers through hers, lining them up until they were in the order he described. "My program sifts those negatives to get these pages and organizes them until they are in the most logical and correct sequence with the most recent views being used."

He covered their joined hands with his free one. "It's time consuming and sometimes there are holes—gaps in the data stream—but we can identify because—"

"Because of the time stamps. You can see when it was opened, what was the last view time and extrapolate?"

"Exactly." He squeezed her hand. "We may not be able to retrieve all of their data, but I've found a lot of the pieces of the puzzle. We've just arranged for a shipment of their defective laptops

—damaged by flood or crushing—back here and we're going to see what, if any, data we can recover and then we'll use the sifting program to manage what we find."

"That's amazing." Warmth stole up her arm, the strength in his hands buffeting her, and she squeezed his hand lightly where their fingers intertwined. "You can really 'rebuild' them?"

"Yeah. Like I said, it won't be perfect and there will be holes they have to fill in the gaps for, but they do a lot of business in the United States and have to file finance reports here. We're investigating how much of the missing information might be in those reports. They've also networked their back up servers and if they back up data in Japan, it's mirrored here in the States to prevent future disaster."

"And I thought you made advanced versions of the shoe comparison program." She may not understand the intricacies of programming, but she could appreciate the attention to detail and amount of review it would take to sort through every single piece of data.

"We do that too."

"Omelets are ready in the dining room." Theresa stood in the doorway, a wistful, watchful expression on her face as she looked at their joined hands. Alyx would have pulled away at the intrusion, discomfort sliding through her, but Daniel tightened his fingers.

"Thank you, Theresa." He slid Alyx's feet off his lap and stood, tugging her to her own feet and still, he held on to her hand. "Shall we?"

"Sure." She fought the discomfort and pasted a smile on. "I have another question about the data."

"Hit me." He pulled her hand up and tucked into the crook of his elbow, holding it captive. They walked side by side, the raw heat of him pushing against her with every step. The contact's disconcerting effect on her equilibrium was hard to ignore.

"Okay, you said the data on the ring fingers were two pages in the same sequence, but what if a fingernail is missing?" She grimaced at the mental image. "If that makes any sense."

"It makes perfect sense." In the dining room, he released her hand only long enough to pull out her chair. It was set for two—omelets, fresh biscuits and crispy home-fried potatoes filled each plate. Glasses of water and orange juice sat on the upper right while a fresh coffee-filled carafe sat perfectly between two empty, clean mugs.

He waited until he sat down and shook out his napkin to finish. "The fingernail may represent two or three lines of data that was not present in the information we found on my ring finger or on yours, but if the data is consecutive enough, they can figure out the missing pieces. If not, we look for alternate images on other machines, and filter for those missing cells."

Unfolding her own napkin slowly, she frowned. "Do you have to review each piece of data to know what to look for?"

"Not exactly. The program does it. It can catalog and identify the cell numbers, every piece has a unique identifier that we can enter as an *if-then* statement." He salted his potatoes before cutting into the omelet.

"Okay, that means if you want blue shoes, and three-inch heels come after one-inch heels, you know that two-inch heels have to come between them or are missing when you review the final product?" Not everything came down to shoes, but it was the first analogy she could think of. The scent of peppers, onions, ham and cheese teased her nostrils and her stomach growled. She took the time to cut into the omelet and steal a bite. Her mouth watered.

Perfect.

She caught him staring at her, a small smile on his lips. "Exactly."

Okay, maybe programming wasn't that hard after all. She grinned.

"Thank you," he murmured and took another bite.

She washed down hers with a drink of orange juice. The cold, tart liquid braced her against the flip-flop of her heart. "For what?"

"For being curious. Not a lot of people ask what I do or when they do, they glaze over if I explain it. So, thank you."

"Well, you're very welcome. I may not understand it all, but you explain it very well."

"Shoe analogies and all?" he teased and she couldn't help laughing.

"I like shoes."

"Nothing wrong with that." He picked up his glass. "To shoes."

Her laughter bubbled up. "To bits and bytes and fingertips and all the other missing pieces you bring home."

Their glasses clinked together and she relaxed. The day seemed a bit brighter too.

∽

DANIEL

A book slammed into the floor with a thump and her *"son of a bitch"* echoed through the hall. Curious, he stood and stretched. The program code he tried to debug wasn't cooperating. Neck cracking as he rolled it from side to side, he crossed his office to glance out at the living room where Alyx stood in the center of the room, an encyclopedia in her hands. She faced off against Victor, her expression a grimace of distaste.

"It's going to break my foot if it keeps falling." She'd changed since the morning and wore a halter-topped dress and sling-back heels, both in a forest-green shade. The color accented her golden tan and brought out the highlights in her red hair.

"Then don't drop it. When a princess walks, she floats with a casual grace that must seem effortless. You can't roll your hips or shake your assets, but rather draw the eye with ethereal grace."

Daniel's gaze roamed over her. She looked more likely to hit Victor with the book in question than to float with grace.

"Again," Victor ordered in a tone that brooked no argument. She sighed, but set the book back on her head. Her shoulders pushed back, her chin came up and she began to walk. He knew the moment she became aware of him. Her soft brown eyes widened, and a falter hitched her step. The book wobbled and Daniel held his breath.

She walked toward him—no. She *glided* forward. Her shoes barely clicked against the tile, each step floating a little more than the last. He locked his jaw, fingers crossing mentally, but when she paused in front of him he grinned. "Very nice."

"Acceptable." But this time, Victor sounded pleased.

She ducked her head and caught the book as it slid off her hair, mussing the strands falling toward her eyes. "Thank you."

"You're welcome." He folded his arms and leaned against the doorjamb. His palms itched to stroke her face.

Or at least give her a hug.

Better to stand his ground and not do either. He teetered close to breaking their contract far more than he liked. It was one thing to play a role, but a part of him didn't feel like he was pretending anymore. "Do I get to see you walk away the same?"

"Excellent idea," Victor agreed. With her back still to her coach, she crossed her eyes and stuck her tongue out at Daniel.

He grinned. "Go on. One more pass and I think you've got the hang of it."

Exhaling a long breath, she balanced the encyclopedia on her head again and pivoted a slow turn on the ball of her foot. Daniel glanced at Victor and found the man watching her every step nearly as hard as he was. The dress flowed around her legs. His gaze skimmed upward, her ass didn't rock from side to side, but it didn't have to. The almost dainty movements gave it a far more provocative sway.

His chest tightened as she reached Victor and paused, her posture near perfect. Holding his breath, he waited for the coach's judgment.

Victor gave her a brief nod. "Acceptable. Tomorrow, we will practice with the taller heels."

"That's it?" Daniel frowned. "You don't tell her great job, give her an applause, just a clipped 'acceptable'?" She deserved a reward, she'd been in here with the man all afternoon, walking, walking, walking.

They both stared at him, Alyx in surprise and Victor with a bemused expression. "Very well. Why don't you take her out to dinner this evening? Somewhere on the beach, a quiet place. That will give you a chance to reward her properly."

"Okay. I will. You looked beautiful, Alyx. Very graceful. Would you allow me to take you out to dinner? We can escape all the rules and—"

Victor cleared his throat. "Actually, it will not be an escape from the rules. It will be your first opportunity to dine in public and we should take full advantage of the intimate situation."

Alyx ducked her head, catching the encyclopedia. "Of course we should."

Instead of rewarding her, he'd just created more work. Daniel sighed. Still, Cinnabars was a lovely beachfront bistro and restaurant. They could eat on the deck, enjoy the ocean breeze and, if he called ahead, he could ask the restaurant to give them some privacy. He could salvage the situation.

"You're ready, Your Highness," Victor encouraged her in a quiet voice. "We'll pick out the perfect dress and shoes. Then all you have to remember is to walk with grace, hold hands and enjoy your meal."

"Absolutely." But her tight smile suggested she didn't share his confidence.

"I'll take care of the arrangements." Daniel straightened. "Be sure to take a break and you can nap if you like." He ignored Victor's raised eyebrows. The man was brilliant, but he was also a slave driver. "The car will pick us up at six."

"Okay."

The tension tightening the corners of her mouth relaxed and Daniel headed back to his home office. He shut the laptop on the program and picked up the phone.

First night out in public or not, he planned for it to be special.

"Christian." He greeted the host by name when the man answered the phone. "Daniel Voldakov here, I need to make some arrangements for a very special dinner this evening..."

CHAPTER 10
ALYX

Alyx smoothed her hand over the dress. It was pure white, a color she would never have—and hadn't—chosen for herself. The strapless gown cupped her breasts and lifted them in a fashion that was both sexy and modest. The drape in the front fell to her knees while the fuller skirt in the back skimmed her ankles. Thank God the silver shoes wrapped around her calves to create a longer leg illusion.

She left her hair down, preferring to have some sort of cover for her bare shoulders. Glimpsing Victor's critical expression in the mirror, his small smile gave her confidence a boost. "Very nice. It's chaste, sweet, and begs the public to wonder more."

"No jewelry?" Surprise flooded her. After all, Victor had entered with four different boxes of gems to choose from. Chokers, teardrop earrings and chains in various shades of gold and platinum, in addition to a wider selection of gems from diamonds to emeralds and rubies.

"The engagement ring only. The location is outdoors. Your dress is summer, warm and casual, but with just enough formality to suggest money, class and style. If it were a black-tie affair, we could dress it up with gems. But tonight, I think simpler is better." He stacked up the velvet boxes. "Don't forget your shawl. It can be chilly after sunset when the ocean breeze turns."

"I won't—and Victor?" She crossed to the closet and drew out the lightly tasseled silken confection that wouldn't keep out a stiff breeze, but still looked elegant.

"Yes, Your Imperial Highness?" The corner of his mouth quirked and Alyx couldn't help smiling in return. After just a few days, the title didn't shock her as it used to.

"Thank you...for everything. I know I'm not the best student, but I appreciate the attention to detail. I won't disappoint you tonight." He made her walk for hours, put her through rigorous tests on protocol and reminded her about her expression continuously, but he also seemed willing to trust her to handle the public dinner tonight.

"You're very welcome, Your Imperial Highness." His heels actually clicked together and he bowed his head before he left. She draped the shawl over her arm and stared after him. Running a hand over her stomach, she looked back at her appearance in the mirror.

A stranger gazed back at her. A stranger possessing her eyes and maybe a hint of her smile. Lifting her chin, she quieted the smile. A princess only beamed when she was on display. A muted tilt to her lips was more appropriate—more serious.

Composed, collected and confident were the catchwords for the night.

"You can do this," she told herself seriously. "It's just a dinner."

A dinner with Daniel—a man she'd shared many meals with and a bedroom—yes, she was on the sofa and he in the bed. She lived in his home; she split ice cream with him at night and discussed the day over coffee every morning.

Why, then, did this feel like a first date?

Inspired, she took a picture of herself in the mirror and sent it to Rhonda with "proof of life" comment. She didn't make me wait for a response, she sent me a laughing face followed by "hawt!"

Shaking her head at herself, she pulled her gaze from the mirror. He waited for her downstairs and it was time to take this princess out for a spin.

Taking a deep breath, she collected her clutch purse from the bed and walked out of the room and paused at the top of the staircase. She teetered for the barest of moments and with more grace and poise than she felt, she laid her hand on the banister and used it for balance as she descended the wide sloping steps.

Halfway down, she caught Daniel's gaze. He stood in the entry hall watching her. Dressed in a button-down shirt, open at the collar, and a dark jacket that matched his slacks, he looked positively rakish. His full mouth tugged upward into a smile and his gaze swept her over from head to toe, approval radiating in his eyes.

She barely remembered her lipstick in time to keep from creasing the color with her teeth. "I hope I didn't keep you waiting."

His hands were in his pockets, and he shook his head slowly. "Not at all, and damn—I would have waited all night for this. You look fantastic."

Warmth radiated through her from the compliment. She dropped her gaze briefly. She wasn't wearing a lot of accessories and her cosmetics were simple, in tune with the dress. Swallowing, she mustered her courage. "Thank you very much."

At the bottom step, he offered his arm. "You're very welcome. Sorry that a night off turned into more work."

"You know it's okay." His sleeve was soft and warm. She wanted to run her hand up and down the fabric, but she settled for just curling her fingers into it.

"No it's not. I didn't really think about how much work this would be." He guided her to the door and set the security alarm before locking up behind them. Despite the size of the house and the room, he didn't maintain any live-in staff. His black Lexus sat waiting in the curved drive, the engine running. He opened the passenger door and held her hand as she slipped inside. "But I will make it up to you tonight with the best seafood you've ever had."

Her stomach rumbled in appreciation. "I love seafood."

"I know." His grin matched hers and he closed the door gently before circling around to climb into the driver's seat.

"I kind of like that you still drive yourself too." It seemed almost surreal to be gliding down the driveway without any bumping along the way. Her old Volvo bounced over every crack in the road.

"I have a car service." He used a remote to open the gates then close them after pulling through. "But I like driving—it gives me time to think."

"I used to run lines in the car on the way to an audition. I wouldn't let myself look at the script —if there was one. But I would memorize the first half dozen lines and recite them in between stoplights. Then whenever I stopped, I would learn a new set and recite those."

He canted his head, splitting his attention between the traffic and her. "You didn't have a script at my audition until you arrived at the theater."

"Nope. I recited Shakespeare." Delight in the memory. She'd spent six months of her seventh-grade year with Mr. Olsen, a teacher who insisted that when a performer could recite the tongue twisters of Shakespeare in a smooth and conver-sational tone, then that performer could do any-thing. Words she took to heart when she had been forced to bid him adieu and moved on to a different set of foster parents in a different school district.

She knew whole passages from Shakespeare

and when she had nothing else to memorize, she ran those lines over and over again.

"Seriously?" His grin grew.

"Seriously." She pressed her lips together. The urge to smile made her cheeks hurt.

"Like what?" He spared a mild look for the car lurching across lanes to cut them off.

"Like...Shakespeare." Her face warmed, she probably shouldn't have brought the subject up, but he'd started it by telling her what he liked to do in the car.

"Would you recite some for me?" They were picking up speed as traffic thinned out toward the coast.

She exhaled, watching him from the corner of her eye. "You don't really want to hear me recite Shakespeare."

"Sure I do." His tone a husky tease. "Go on. You can't tell me you have Shakespeare memorized enough to recite in the car and then not show me."

Exasperation mingled with pleasure at his interest. Folding her arms, she leaned into the seat and tilted her head to look at him. "This can be no trick. The conference was sadly borne. They have the truth of this from Hero. They seem to pity the lady, it seems her affections have their full bent." The words rolled off her tongue, gathering force and emotion.

Daniel nodded and motioned with his right hand for her to continue.

"Love me?" She hesitated, locking gazes with him for a heartbeat. "Why, it must be requited."

She turned her head away and looked to watch the ocean out the window. "I hear how I am censored. They say I will bear myself proudly if I perceive the love come from her. They say too that she will rather die than give any sign of affection. I did never think to marry. I must not seem proud. Happy are they that hear their detractions and can put them to mending."

She paused, stealing a glance at his profile. His grin diminished to the barest of smiles curving his lips and his attention continued to divert from the traffic to look at her. "Is there more?" he asked.

"Of course." She toyed with the shawl over her arm, her fingers plucking at the fabric.

"Have at it, then."

"You really want to hear the speech?"

"Yes, I really want to hear the speech." He tapped the steering wheel. "Ticktock."

Laughter bubbled up inside her and she relaxed her grip on the shawl. "*They say the lady is fair. Tis truth, I can bear witness. And virtuous.*" She extended a hand palm-up. "*'Tis so I cannot reprove it. Wise, but for loving me. By my troth, it is no addition to her wit nor no great argument of her folly, for I will be horribly in love with her.*"

Curling her fingers into a fist, she pressed her hand to her chest just above the strapless bodice. "*I may chance have some odd quirks and remnants of wit broken on me because I have railed so long against marriage, but doth not the appetite alter?*" She looked at him questioningly. His nod both surprised and delighted her. "*A man loves the meat in his youth that he cannot endure in his age. Shall quips and sentences and these paper bullets of the brain awe a man from the career of his humor? No. The world must be peopled.'"* She struck her fist to the flat of her other palm. *"'When I said I would die a bachelor, I did not think I should live till I were married. Here comes Beatrice.'"*

She ended the last with a hushed flourish and pressed her fingers to her lips when Daniel applauded with one hand against the steering wheel. "Bravo, bravo."

He slowed the car and turned into a lot in front of a cozy-looking, wood-hewn building. The valet greeted him at his door with a ticket and a second opened her side of the car. She barely made it to her feet before Daniel swept around to claim her arm and threaded it through his.

They were swiftly shown out onto a deck that overlooked the ocean. The view took her breath away. The water rolled in, foaming gently to lap against the rocky sand below. The sun dipped lower on the western horizon, adding a spectacular array of red, gold and amber to the evening. Surprisingly, the deck was empty save for the two of them and their waitress, who sat them at a table, meant for four, right at the very edge of the deck.

The unencumbered horizon stretched out and she forgot the server was there as she stared across the water.

"Would you care for some wine to begin the evening?"

"That would be lovely—red or white, darling?" The affectation pulled her back to herself and their surroundings more swiftly than ice being poured down her back.

She started to say red, but a glance at her dress and she changed her mind. "White would be lovely." The last thing she needed was a fat red stain on the very new—very expensive—dress.

"White for both of us. California vintage preferred." Daniel waited until the waitress left to fetch the wine and grinned. "Do you always quote *Othello*, or other plays?"

Her eyes widened. "There's no Beatrice in *Othello*."

"Oh, was that *Romeo and Juliet*?" He looked perplexed.

"No." She shook head and leaned forward, the menu shaking with her barely suppressed humor. "It's *Much Ado About Nothing*."

"Oh." Daniel shrugged and flipped his menu open. "I didn't think that one could have much in it, considering the 'nothing' subject matter."

She gaped until she saw the quirk of a smile he tried to hide behind the menu. She laughed. "You're terrible."

"Guilty." He paused as the waitress returned with the wine glasses and the wine. She took her time in opening the bottle for them and poured a sample. When Daniel gave her an approving nod following his taste, she filled both glasses half-full.

"Would you like to hear the specials?"

At his quirked brows, Alyx shook her head. She knew what she wanted already. "I'm going to have the lobster-and-shrimp linguini in Alfredo sauce." The calories would be killer, but it was her favorite and the sauce matched her dress.

"Make that two." He collected the menus and passed them to the waitress.

"I'll be right back with your salad and bread." The waitress disappeared and Alyx frowned at the growing crowd inside. The weather on the deck was next to perfect, cool breeze, still warm sun and the lull of the ocean.

"What's wrong?"

"Nothing, I just think it's odd that they look busy in there and it's quiet out here. I expected a lot more people would want to eat outside with this view." She picked up her wineglass and took a sip. It was cold, crisp and carried just the right amount of bite. She would have to check the bottle later. Her preference for red wine aside, this vintage tasted quite good.

"I'm sure they do. I'm sorry they can't be accommodated." He took a swallow of his wine, then leaned back in the chair, a smug look on his face.

She set the glass down. "What did you do?"

"I promised you an evening off. Victor wanted us to show off. We can do both. Private dinner, private deck—call it a golden compromise."

After she absorbed that piece of knowledge, her eyes widened, and so did her smile. "You realize that's cheating."

"Not really. I made you a promise—I wanted to keep it. They can still see us out here—and they can wonder just who is that beautiful, beautiful woman and the lucky SOB sitting across from her."

Warmth flooded her face again and she hid her discomfort with another drink. Of course, the mystique would be perfect—particularly for the curious. They were putting on a show, after all. "Positively brilliant."

She admired the cunning nature of the plan. As test runs went, she only had to look the part— and the dress did most of the work for her. They quieted as the waitress brought the salads and the bread. Unwrapping her utensils from the cloth napkin, she refused to look to her left. She didn't want to know if anyone stared at them— or if the plan he'd carefully executed worked.

"Good?" he asked after she took a bite of the salad.

"It's very good." She nodded, not really tasting any of the lettuce. Oddly enough, the bright sunshine of the evening seemed to dim before the sun had fully set. The cool breeze ruffling her back left chills in its wake. Even the wine went a little sour on her tongue. But she mustered her smile and focused on her "date."

She'd forgotten the cardinal rule of make-believe.

None of this is real.

And she really didn't have the right to be disappointed.

CHAPTER 11

DANIEL

"You're on the front cover of the social section, stud. And your princess looks pretty hot. Nice job." Martin'd apparently took Daniel's advice to heart and got on board. His compliment buzzed through Daniel's sleep-fogged brain.

"Why are we on the front cover of the social section?" Three nights in a row he'd taken her out for dinner—choosing private, secluded locations to let her relax and show off without having to work. Victor gave him some grief, since the point was to be seen, but he didn't care. The acting coach arrived early every morning to begin a new round of lessons. Whether it was cosmetics, walking, talking or sitting, Alyx worked her sweet, curvy little ass off. Dinner was the only reward he could give her for the moment.

"Apparently, you were seen dining together two nights in a row—and I'm quoting the article here—'...looks like self-made software magnate Daniel Voldakov is off the market, ladies. Too bad you didn't grab the chance when you had it. Who is the mysterious beauty seen on Voldakov's arm? Rumor has it that Voldakov's royal taste is impeccable.'"

Sitting up, Daniel scrubbed a hand over his face and stared at the tousled blankets on the sofa. His back ached in a twinge of sympathy. She really needed to stop sleeping there. As hard as she worked during the day, it couldn't be good for her.

"You still listening?" Martin verbally poked him over the phone.

"Yeah, sorry. I was on with Takahashi until four this morning, but it looks like this last round is doing exactly what they need."

"Did he say yes to the contract?" Enthusiasm welled beneath the question.

"Not in so many words." Shoving back the bedsheets, he swung out of bed and padded over to the sofa. He collected the pillow and blanket and added them to the disarray of the bed. Tonight, he had another long conference call and he would swap spots with her.

"Damn, I thought saving their bacon would give you that foothold."

"I didn't say he said no." Daniel grinned, glad his best friend couldn't see him. "I believe the phrase he used was that he would be honored to discuss the matter in person in Los Angeles in one week."

"Hot damn." The echo of Martin's hand slapping against a desktop underscored the words.

"The CEO wouldn't meet you personally unless he was ready to sign the papers."

"I'm aware." Putting the phone on speaker, he set it to the side of the sink and turned on the water. Splashing his face, he then lathered shaving cream on his jaw. "I'll talk to Lucy. Takahashi will be here in six days. I need to clear my schedule."

"You know that might be a great time to introduce him to your princess." Speculation ran rampant under the words. "Privately and then, of course, publicly."

Daniel hesitated, razor poised. Teasing the press with sightings was one thing, but taking her out and actively putting her on display? Daniel wasn't sure he was ready for that. The point was to lure the grand duke into conversation, into opening doors—but the Japanese contract could definitely bait the hook for the EU. "I don't know," he hedged and concentrated on gliding the razor over his cheeks, stripping off the overnight growth of stubble. Dark circles ringed his eyes. The lack of sleep was bound to catch up with him.

"You sleeping with her yet?"

He nicked himself and bit back a curse. "No."

"You must be losing your touch. She cleans up real well, and talk about a sweet package."

Rinsing the razor, Daniel glared at the phone. "Martin, stop looking at her package and get your mind back on business. Start a draft of the contract we want from Takahashi, but be ready to flex the details."

"Already drafted."

After dabbing the nick with a washcloth, he finished shaving. "Your confidence is showing."

"Well, I knew you were a great bet when you wrote those algorithms in college and CalTech featured you at their software symposium."

Washing the remnants of the lather off his face, Daniel shook his head. "I'll see you later this afternoon."

"Yup. See you." Martin hung up and Daniel stared at himself in the mirror. If Takahashi signed the deal, Spherecast had its entry into the Japanese market. The loyalty and honor shown by their corporation required personal attention to detail, but the business software was just the first step.

Games would come next.

He ducked through a quick shower, toweled off and had just pulled on his pants when a knock preceded Alyx's entry into the room. Dressed in jeans and a billowy shirt, with her hair hanging loosely, she looked like a bohemian escapee rather than a princess. But one sniff of the fresh coffee she held out to him and a thrill went through him. She'd brought *him* coffee.

"Good morning. You're a little underdressed for Victor, aren't you?" Not that Daniel minded, but the coach demanded a very specific look from the princess they were building. He cradled the cup and took the first welcome drink of the coffee. It was the first time she'd reciprocated his offers of coffee first thing in the morning, but with his late-night meeting schedule, she was often up long before he could deliver it.

"Victor can't be here today. He called a little while ago to apologize." Her nose wrinkled and she dropped her voice as though imitating the man. "We shall resume my education tomorrow."

She had the day off.

He mentally reviewed his schedule. He could juggle a few items around and take it with her. "Want to do something fun?"

"I still have homework."

He waved a hand. "What? Read more Russian history? It's bloody and it's tragic and best served with a lot of vodka. Trust me." He'd heard it all from his immigrant grandfather. The stories didn't get better with age—they just got sadder.

"Something like that. He wants me to memorize the family tree so I can quote who it is I'm supposed to be related to."

Zeroing in on the "supposed to be," Daniel frowned. "You *are* related to them, sweetheart." He didn't know where the endearment came from. It just slipped right off his tongue. Startling how natural that seemed.

"Okay, there's related and then there's *related*." She shook her head and carried her coffee over to the sofa, curling up on one corner of it. The morning sunshine was a perfect complement to the red in her hair. She looked both delicate and delectable.

Have you slept with her yet? Martin's question rang through his mind and he pushed the lascivious thoughts that accompanied it away. She'd made the no-sex rule clear. He would respect it. Sitting on the corner of the bed, he studied her. "And the difference is?"

"If you met a man tomorrow whose father and your father were related, which would then make you two relatives—is he automatically family to you? Or just some guy on the street who happens to share some DNA strands?" She followed her question with a sip of coffee, her gaze somber and serious.

It was a fair question. He took a swallow of the hot brew. "That's not an easy question to answer. Yes, we would be cousins of some sort. But he's still a stranger."

"Exactly, so all those people that I'm supposed to be related to. They're names in a book—grainy pictures on the web. They are reels and videos on TikTok or meme'd to death. I don't *know* them and they certainly don't *know* me. It's like studying for a history test. It should mean something, but it doesn't." Despite her easy manner, he heard the pensive note in her voice.

"Well, do any of them look like your father? Resemblance is a key to imprinting for some. My dad looked like his dad and I look like them. I see myself when I look at the family."

"I don't know." She shrugged and the sadness in her voice crept into her eyes. "I barely remember what my father looked like anymore. I try—but it's like an out-of-focus image."

His chest tightened. "You don't have any pictures?"

Lips tight, she shook her head slowly. "No. I

wasn't allowed to take much with me when I went into the system. Only what was necessary and I could carry. There was a fire when I was twelve—or maybe it was thirteen? Mrs. Johnson. Sweet lady, but a terrible cook." A bittersweet humor turned up the corners of her mouth. "She was trying to wrangle kids and get dinner ready. The stove top caught on fire and she tried to douse it with water, but it was a grease fire."

Daniel winced. Pour water on a grease fire and it spreads faster. "Alyx, I'm sorry."

"It's okay." Her little shrug belied the words. "My room was right over the top of the kitchen. When the fire went up the wall, I lost most of my stuff. I didn't really care about the clothes, and I've never had very many things, but I'd left the photo album on the bed."

She didn't mention the beaten-up bear in her car, but he was glad that hadn't been consumed in the fire. "They couldn't salvage any?"

"Nope." She lifted her coffee mug in rueful salute. "Most of them were from before digital got popular and they'd never been scanned in to anything. There were entire envelopes of negatives and they melted. I was upset, but in a month I was on to my next foster and there wasn't much else I could do. My caseworker tried to track down some pictures for me, but then she was reassigned and my new caseworker was a harried, overworked guy with a lot of problems. Finding old pictures just didn't seem to qualify. We were too busy finding me the right place to sleep."

The foster system needed a lot of work. The staff was underpaid, the children numerous and real long-term homes an elusive myth for many of the kids. Knowing that intellectually and seeing the raw evidence in the pain she tried to hide were completely different. Sitting forward, elbows on his knees, he made a decision.

"Forget the homework for today. You were born in Woodland."

She lifted her eyebrows. "Yeah."

"Your parents' house was there. What happened to all the stuff in it? I mean they had to have furniture, knickknacks, possessions of some kind."

"I don't know. No one really said anything to me about the house or the stuff in it, just that I had to pack a bag." She waved a hand, as though trying to clear a cobweb from the air in front of her. "And it doesn't matter. It was years ago. What things they might have had were probably sold or dragged off."

He didn't miss the crease of tension knitting her brows together. "Well, we can find out. It's a short flight to Sacramento. We rent a car and we go look."

"We can't just fly to Sacramento." She lowered the coffee cup and gaped at him,

Decided, he stood and finished his own drink before setting the cup on the dresser. "Why not?"

"Because you have a job and I have homework to do."

"No, I have a company, which means I make the rules, and I just decided to give myself the day off. You have homework to learn more about your family. I think finding out what happened to your house and your stuff qualifies." He walked into the closet before she could respond then returned with a shirt. After tugging it on, he went looking for his phone.

"But what about your Japanese deal? I know you were up with them late last night."

True, and he'd been exhausted when he first woke up. But this was a problem he could solve and if he couldn't get her all the answers, she deserved to have someone looking for the pieces so she could put them back together. "My deal is fine. The software is debugged and working well within the parameters they require. They're rebuilding their database. Let's go rebuild yours— besides, I know this great Italian place. We can get Stromboli so good that your mouth will water and your eyes weep."

He traded out the work slacks for a more comfortable pair of jeans and grabbed a well-worn pair of sneakers. Wallet in his back pocket, keys in the front. She was still sitting on the sofa when he sat down to pull on some socks.

"Move it, Alyx. Get some shoes. We can get breakfast on the way to the airport." He speed-dialed Lucy and tucked the phone between his shoulder and ear. "Good morning and yes, I know it's before office hours. I'll put a fifty in the jar. Can you get me two tickets to Sacramento on the first available flight that leaves within—" he juggled to glance at his watch, "—the next ninety minutes? If there aren't any, just charter me a plane for the day."

"Of course, Daniel. Name of your passenger?"

"Alyx Dagmar." Socks on, he pulled on a shoe and began lacing it up. He motioned with his eyes for Alyx to get moving and she finally scooted off the sofa. Her clothes and shoes were still in her own room.

He would have a word with Theresa about making some room in his closet. She shouldn't have to dart back and forth between rooms.

"I've got you booked on a hopper that leaves in eighty-five minutes. I've done remote check-in and sent the boarding passes to your phone. Anything else?" Lucy's dry voice dragged him back to the present.

"Yep, cancel my appointments for the day and let Martin know I'm going to be unreachable. I'll check in with you tomorrow."

"Really?" The stutter in her voice was very un-Lucy.

"Is that so surprising?" He was the boss and he could take a day off if he wanted.

"Frankly, yes. Do you know when the last time was you took any time for yourself?" She sounded proud in her bemusement.

Second shoe tied, he stood and caught the phone before it fell. "Not off the top of my head, but we don't have anything urgent enough to worry about a few hours off the clock."

"No, Daniel. We don't." Lucy's voice gentled. "But it's been two years. Take the day, I'll hold all calls. I think this new lady in your life is good for you."

He paused at those words and cleared his throat. "Thanks. I'll see you tomorrow."

"No rush." He swore he could hear the smile in her words. "Take the rest of the week."

She hung up before he could say anything else and Daniel stared at the phone in his hand. Taking the rest of the week off didn't sound like a bad idea. But first, Sacramento. He knew how to track down lost information in the software world. It was time to help Alyx put together the pieces of her history.

CHAPTER 12
ALYX

Surprisingly—or maybe not that surprising—they sat in first class on a small plane departing LAX for Sacramento. They didn't have to rush through security—Daniel's connections earning them a spot in the exclusive line of frequent travelers and high-end customers. They handed over their driver's licenses, walked through the metal detectors, and were off again. He'd alternated between holding her hand—to keep from getting separated—or laying his palm against her lower back as if to guide her through the lines of humanity streaming in from one gate or rushing off to another.

Daniel turned out to be a terrific traveling companion. He knew all the tricks to weave around the crowds and when the crowd thickened, he charmed a path. At the gate to their flight, he led them right up to the attendant checking in passengers and showed her the boarding passes on his phone and they were whisked up the gangway and into their seats.

Daniel flipped open his laptop as soon as they were in the air, then glanced over at her.

"Do you remember the street address?"

"1710 Bonner Avenue." She never forgot the address or the digits of the family phone number. Her mother'd drilled those into her before kindergarten. With all the addresses she'd had over the years, she'd expected to have forgotten it. But no, she could still picture the white A-frame house, four-foot-white-fenced-in front yard and the driveway with its cracked pavement and grass threading through the seams spider-webbing the concrete. She'd learned to roller skate on that driveway, falling often enough that by the time she mastered it, her bottom ended up bruised and sore.

Her gaze misted at the memory and she cleared her throat, covering the emotion with a quick swallow of orange juice. "It's in Woodland."

"Yep." He opened a browser window and plugged in the address. "Just want to check our drive time. I'll rent a car when we get there." A map scrolled across his screen with their route highlighted in green. "Not bad at all. Hungry?"

The stewardess was heading toward them with muffins. Alyx shook her head, despite the growling cramp in her stomach. The morning rush to race off to the airport on this unexpected journey to the past had knotted her insides. "I'm good. Thanks."

Maybe she should have said no, or at least put up more than a token resistance. This trip had nothing to do with why he hired her, a job she constantly reminded herself about. Leaning back in the seat, she forced herself to look out the window. The California landscape was nowhere near as interesting as her traveling companion. But staring at Daniel had its consequences. Like forgetting he was an employer and they weren't really involved.

A warm hand covered hers. She jumped and glanced to her left. His full, rich mouth turned up in the gentlest of smiles. "It's going to be okay."

Her heart squeezed and her stomach did a little flip-flop.

Damn, it was easy to forget he was her employer.

Too easy.

"Thank you. I'm worried that this is a waste of our time," she lied again—the lie much easier to swallow than the raw truth. "There's a lot of work to do." She carefully avoided mentioning the words *princess* or *practice*. The whimsical trip to Sacramento to track down her childhood home and the slim possibility of finding treasured memories didn't fit anywhere in his future plans.

Despite her very real concern, eagerness clawed at her belly. Would the house be the same color? Would the residents have fixed the driveway? Her father'd wanted to. He'd mentioned it every day when he came home from work—swooping in like some hero to scoop her up and spin her in a circle. She couldn't see his face anymore, but the strength enveloping her in his arms grounded her—filled her with longing. Turning her hand over under Daniel's, she threaded her fingers through his. He tightened his grip and that same sense of protective power swept over her again.

"I know." He gave her another one of those endearing smiles, the kind that socked her in the solar plexus and left warm emotion to flow through her body. Her nipples tightened and she forced her gaze to drop to their joined hands. If she looked into his eyes, he might see past all the barriers to the ragged soul inside. The soul that longed to see her home again and the little girl—buried beneath years of carefully built barriers—who wished her parents would be at the other end of this journey.

Stupid. Stupid. Stupid. The internal voice chided the hopelessly juvenile thoughts. Her parents were dead. They'd died a very long time ago and she'd given up on hoping for a miracle or a fairy tale where they swooped in to find her again.

Why then could she not contain the eagerness flushing through her blood or warming her skin?

"Alyx." Her name rolled off his tongue, heating her like brandy, but a thousand times sweeter and more provocative. "Knowing where we come from, it's important." His head tilted toward her and her throat closed. He was close enough to kiss. The warmth of his breath tickled her cheek. "I can't promise you we'll find anything today, but I want to try. And this isn't about

HEATHER LONG

business or deals—it's just something I want to do."

The kindness and the sense of the purpose in the words were too much. They should be back in Beverly Hills. Victor should be drilling her on how to walk, to talk and to eat in public. Daniel should be barricaded in his study, debugging code. The fantasy they worked on constructing was far safer than this—far safer than sitting here, gripping his hand. This was real.

Too real.

She should let him go, but no matter how much she knew it was a mistake, she couldn't quite bring her fingers to unlock from his.

"Okay." She swallowed, because the whisper was all she could manage.

"Okay." He squeezed her hand and his grin tightened another band around her heart. "Do you want to eat first or drive straight to the address?"

The man seemed determined to fatten her up. Her lips curved. It was altogether too damn sweet. Affection softened her resolve. "Are you hungry?"

"Starved," he admitted, unabashed. He ignored the laptop in front of him, his blue-eyed gaze fixed on her. She made the mistake of staring into those eyes. This would be a lot easier on her equilibrium if he were ugly.

"Then let's get food first." She couldn't stomach the thought of food. The coffee she drank earlier sat like a rock in her belly and the orange juice churned around it, burning like acid.

"Fantastic, I know this great little diner. It's about halfway between the airport and your address. They make waffles, like, this big..." He tugged his hand free to mime a huge circle with both his hands. She fought the disappointment at the loss of contact. Just when she thought her rough emotions were under control, his warm fingers closed on hers again. "Strawberry waffles with whipped cream."

Her stomach growled, a low sound, but unmistakable even with the engine noise. His lips curved teasingly. "I heard that."

"Shh." Her face warmed. "It's not polite."

He laughed and the sound draped around her like a shawl. "Okay, but you're hungry and trust me—the waffles will be worth it."

Not quite trusting the wild tingles racing through her, she nodded slowly. "I believe you."

The answer satisfied him and he leaned back in his seat and flipped his screen to a news site's business feed. He read through the top stories, still cradling her hand in his.

If she closed her eyes, she could almost imagine this was real.

Damn her if she didn't want to do just that.

HE RENTED A LEXUS. A very nice, very comfortable, *sink into the seats and let it cradle the body*, Lexus. The man spent money like some people collected coupons. He didn't look at the receipt when he signed the rental slip. Conversation lagged until he negotiated his way through traffic and put them on the road toward Woodland.

"Nervous?" He tossed a glance her way, but she shook her head.

"No." She intended to leave it at that, but surprised herself. "A little uncertain. We're assuming that the house is still there and that the people in it will have some idea of who lived there before."

Was that why her stomach refused to settle? Why it kept flip-flopping like a fish caught on a line?

"We're not assuming the new owners know anything. I didn't think to have the P.I. investigate the property. He traced the sale of it, but that happened after your parents passed."

Her stomach sank at the reminder, not that she needed one. The last time she'd tried to get answers, she ended up spending a small fortune in calling cards and getting nowhere. She'd finally given up. If the social workers had anything for her, maybe it had all gone to her care with the state.

"But—" he patted her thigh in the most casual and familiar of gestures, "—the area of Woodland you grew up in is known for longevity of its residents. I'm hoping your neighbors remember and can point us in the right direction."

Neighbors. How easily he described them. Neighbors were not something she'd given a thought to or considered a potential source. Her life had revolved around fitting into a new home or a new school, not maintaining ties to a past that grew more distant, almost invisible in the rearview mirror of time.

"We're assuming that my parents were social." It was a lame rebuttal and the patient look he wore tweaked her.

"You don't have to be social to notice your neighbors. When I was seven, we lived in this great little trailer park." He grinned at the grimace she couldn't hide fast enough. "Don't knock trailer parks. They don't always have the best reputation, but I loved living there. I couldn't have told you the names of my neighbors, but I knew them all on sight and they knew me. They'd get after me if I was getting too rambunctious and they were always keeping an eye on the kids in the neighborhood. I went back about four years ago, just out of curiosity, and a lot of them remembered me."

"Yeah?" A nugget of hope edged past the doubt coiling in her belly.

"Hmm-hmm. They remembered the windows I'd broken with my baseballs and the fact that I preferred reading and playing on that 'damn' computer to more manly pursuits. Mrs. Filmore, who taught my third-grade class, still lived in her trailer house across from our old lot and she was impressed that I grew into my brain."

Alyx couldn't help but join in with his laughter. There was something carefree about it. "You grew into your brain?"

"Oh yeah." He leaned back in the seat, the jeans he wore stretching over his muscular thighs. Muscles she couldn't help but notice when he breezed through his bedroom in boxers. The man might work in software, but he knew how to keep fit and trim. She dragged her mind away from imagining him without his pants to focus on the next story. "I was a bit of a smart-ass in school."

"Bit?" She lifted her brows skeptically. He seemed straightforward and sweet, but she enjoyed the acerbic bite to his wit.

"Okay, I was a lot of a smart-ass in school. I could argue my way out of PE on a regular basis and she used to have to let me read when I was done with tests because I always finished with thirty to forty minutes to spare—and the last time I got really bored in her class, I took apart the new computer they'd received to see how the parts worked." He flashed another toothy grin. "I couldn't put it back exactly as I found it."

A fresh wave of laughter threatened to burst from her lips and she shook her head. The ease with which he could make her smile—it undid her. She didn't doubt his tale for an instant. "Was she impressed that you owned your own company?"

He shrugged and slowed the car, turning into a lot next to the most ordinary diner she'd ever seen. It looked straight out of the annals of television history, down to the orange on the sign and the line of booths visible through the wide panel glass windows.

"I don't think that mattered. Money doesn't buy happiness or success." He killed the engine and turned to look at her. "It doesn't buy peace of mind either."

Hard to argue with that. She didn't remember having much money before her parents died and financial concerns didn't faze her through the rest of her teen years until she wanted a car. She'd gotten a job and earned what she needed to buy an old secondhand vehicle from her foster mother at the time. Fortunately, she'd managed to buy it just a month before her move to her final foster home. The car saved her life that year—it was the first time she bought something of tangible value and it had granted her a freedom she hadn't known she craved. Freedom she needed because her last set of foster parents had been on the fast track to early graves. The money they earned by taking in foster kids went directly to their liquor bills. They liked their charges older, because ignoring them didn't mean much and most, like her, knew better than to stir up the crap with them. She'd learned quick that weekends were better spent staying away from that house. The car let her do it.

Still musing on that, she slid out of the rental and followed him. She avoided taking his hand again, no matter how much her palm itched for the contact. The familiarity and comfort he seemed to have developed in touching her left her quivering on the inside. It was better to put in a little distance for now. At the door to the diner, she paused. Blinking twice, she read the name written in white letters.

It couldn't be right.

"The Snooty Pig?"

Daniel's grin grew and he grasped the door with one hand and slid the other against her lower back. Her skin tingled beneath the shirt. "Yep. You'll not get a better bacon-and-eggs breakfast anywhere. But the waffles—the waffles are to die for."

"There's something vaguely wrong with that statement." Unable to suppress her amusement, she grinned back at him. Inside, the diner was exactly as she expected—vinyl seats, Formica-topped tables and waitresses in aproned uniforms. If some salty waitress sailed out with a "kiss my grits" apron she wouldn't have been surprised. They claimed a table near the window and reviewed the menus. Everything was served with home fries or hash browns. The air was scented with coffee, bacon, sausage and ham. Cups clinked against tables and forks scraped on plates.

She picked out a waffle immediately, but decided against the strawberries and whipped cream. Her hips didn't need any assistance... Besides, butter and syrup sounded better. Daniel made a face at her as he ordered extra whipped cream and a double side of bacon to share.

The waitress left them with their fresh coffee and for the first time since their impromptu jaunt began, she found herself without anything to say —and that was okay too. Because she enjoyed sipping her coffee and splitting her attention between the diner patrons and Daniel.

His leg slid against hers and relaxed. That

simple contact sent her heart racing, but eased the tension in her shoulders.

"Thank you." She set her coffee cup down and folded her hands together on the cool Formica.

"For what?"

"For this—the trip, the interest in my family." Maybe he was interested in her royal roots, but a trip to Woodland, California, wasn't about her so-called ties to some Russian nobility. It was about her parents. About the life she'd lived before they died and a past she'd nearly forgotten. "You didn't have to do this. It's not really going to help your business and I know that. So, thank you."

He propped his chin against a fist and stared at her. His easy smile faded and his sharp blue eyes sobered. "Alyx, you're a friend. All that other stuff aside—I like to think we are becoming friends. And I help my friends."

His solemn gaze trapped her, and fear skittered up her spine. "Really?"

"Yeah, really. Look, Alyx—"

Whatever else he might have said was interrupted by the waffles. Her eyes grew at the sight of the strawberries and whipped cream piled on top of his, all but hiding it from sight.

"Wow." Hers came with a mini scoop of butter in the center and a little pitcher of syrup. Her stomach let out a growl and it seemed she was hungrier than she thought.

His expression hardened briefly, as though irritated by the interruption, but it smoothed away and his relaxed smile returned. "Yes, it looks like dessert—I'd think a woman would appreciate dessert before dinner." He scooped up a forkful of the decadent breakfast and held it out to her temptingly. "You sure you don't want to try it?"

She wasn't sure who was more surprised when she opened her mouth and took the bite. If the tart and sweet mixture of waffle, fruit and sweet cream didn't mingle on her tongue in an explosively sensual tease of her palate, the delighted smile softening the hard glint in his eyes would have. "Mmm—fantastic."

"I told you." He cut himself another bite and she couldn't help but watch his tongue as he caught a bit of whipped cream that escaped across his lips. "Want more?"

Her imagination must have run away from reality, because the loaded question seemed to hint beyond the offer of another bite. Catching her lower lip in her teeth, she shook her head slowly. "No, thank you."

Disappointment dimmed his smile, but only for a moment. He slipped another forkful past his lips.

She envied that fork.

Get a grip, she ordered herself and forced her gaze to her own breakfast and cut into it with only a sliver of the interest she'd experienced watching him eat. *Friends is one thing. I can do friends. We can be friends.*

Yeah. She was in so much trouble.

CHAPTER 13
DANIEL

D aniel couldn't remember the last time he'd had so much fun over a meal.

He'd actually managed to tempt her into another bite of the strawberry waffle. The whipped cream on the corner of her mouth had left him aching to clean it away for her, but her pink tongue slipped out and took away his excuse. By the time they climbed back into the car, their conversation shifted to tunes and she argued for control of the music. He insisted on using his phone. That was before she declared his music list hopeless and downloaded a Pandora app.

She erased all his complaints when Katy Perry started playing and she danced in her seat. Like the Madonna lyrics, she knew these too. He'd never been a fan of pop music, but Alyx rapidly revised his opinion. He followed the GPS instructions toward the address where she grew up, but the closer they came, the more dilapidated the neighborhood seemed to be.

It wasn't until he pulled on to her street that he regretted the impulsive journey.

Halfway down the block he stopped the car next to the curb and fought the urge to curse. No houses remained. Nothing of a neighborhood was visible. Instead, a national chain's superstore occupied a huge lot with a strip mall's worth of little stores jutting out from each side.

He felt more than saw Alyx deflate. She turned away to look out the window, absorbing the scene.

"I'm sorry." Two of the lamest words on the planet folded together, offering paltry compensation.

"It's okay." But the emptiness in her tone gave lie to that phrase.

"No, it's not." He leaned against the steering wheel and glared at the blacktopped parking lots and the sunlight bouncing off the cars. Why the hell didn't he check with the P.I.? Copies of the news articles about her parents' deaths had been in the files and he could have sworn there were photos of the house—but now he had to wonder if they were older images the investigator found.

"It's okay, Daniel." Her shoulders lifted and she folded her arms across her chest as she sat back in the seat. Gone was the loose bounce of her foot and nod of her head to the music. Her expression tightened, turning her lips down in a pensive frown. "Really. We should probably just head back to Los Angeles. I can get some more work done."

Maybe that's what they should do, but her

touch-me-not aura aggravated him almost as much as the strip mall. "We're not done. We could go down to social services and talk to them about your file."

He plugged in the request to his phone, searching for a social services office in the area. It made sense that she would have gone into local foster custody before she began the pattern of bouncing from home to home.

"It's not important." The dullness of those words scraped over his nerves. "Really. We've already wasted a lot of time—not to mention money—on this."

"My money to waste." He didn't mean to snap but it wasn't a waste. *Dammit.* He focused on the phone's GPS. The social services office was just ten blocks away—if the damn thing was still there. "And my time."

"I forgot. You're the boss." The retreat turned into a full rout. Daniel cut a glance sideways at her, but she didn't look at him. He touched a hand to her leg, the gesture almost tentative after the ease of earlier. But when she stiffened further, he backed off. Both hands on the steering wheel, he turned them around and followed the phone's instructions.

Twenty cold minutes later, he pulled up in front of the nondescript and altogether depressing concrete building with Child Protection Services printed on the glass door in block letters. He slid out of the car and waited in the cool sunshine. He thought she was going to let him fend for himself, but after three long minutes, she stepped out, her normally expressive face fixed in a cool, detached mask.

She followed him to the door and he managed to grab the handle and open it a second before she did.

The office smelled like feet. Worn carpet and split vinyl demonstrated that the agency's funds certainly didn't cover their interiors. The noise level climbed exponentially and stacks of paper littered the myriad of desks forming a horseshoe beyond the receptionist. An older woman looked up at them with a careworn expression but sharp eyes.

"Can I help you?" The brisk tone ordered him to make it quick and not waste her time.

"You can." He leaned an elbow on the counter and gave the receptionist a charming smile. "We're here for the personal items of Alyx Dagmar. She would have been entered into the system sixteen years ago. Most of her belongings were not taken with her when she was placed."

White eyebrows knitted together. "Sixteen years ago? And who are you?"

"Yes, sixteen years ago. I'm Daniel Voldakov." He pulled out his ID and handed it to her. "And this is my fiancée, Alyx Dagmar."

He glanced over his shoulder in time to catch Alyx wince at the word fiancée. But she pulled out her own ID and passed it over.

The receptionist scanned both cards and looked past Daniel to Alyx. "You don't remember me, do you, sweetie?"

Alyx moved closer, almost brushing his arm,

but shifting at the last minute to avoid contact. She studied the older woman. "I'm sorry." She shook her head. "I don't."

"Well, that's to be expected. I was there the night they came to tell you about your parents. Probably best that you don't have a crystal-clear memory of that." She handed their IDs back. Her face wrinkled in a gentle smile.

"You weren't my representative, though." The question in Alyx's voice betrayed her uncertainty.

"No, unfortunately, we were massively overloaded. I was just here when the call came in. I picked you up and stayed with you that first night. You were Susanna Fraser's after that. But Susanna—oh, she left for the private sector nearly—"

"Ten years and six months ago." Alyx finished the sentence for her. "I remember. She promised to get some of my things together, but the next week it was Mr. Daughtry and he didn't have time for it."

"Him. Yes. He never had time for much." The older woman rubbed her chin. "You should have been given your boxes when you turned eighteen."

"My boxes?" The stiffness in Alyx's shoulders relaxed some. "What boxes?"

Pushing her chair back, the white-haired woman motioned to another harried worker. "Cynthia? Watch the front for me. I want to take these two into a client room." She disappeared around the side and a door buzzed, admitting them to the chaos of the work area. Daniel held the door, careful not to touch Alyx lest she really pull away. He trailed after her as they walked through the cubicles and down to a small conference room.

It was more dismal than the rest of the office, if that was possible. He ignored the plastic chairs, and took a position against the wall and waited. This was about her and he didn't want to push her by playing their charade any further in the office. She looked so damned uncomfortable as she perched on the edge of one of the seats.

"I'm sorry, but I don't remember your name." Alyx half-rose again when the older woman returned and pulled out a chair for herself.

"It's Grace, Grace Burrows. Don't worry about that. Sit." She flipped open a digital tablet and touched a few buttons. "This will take me a moment. We just upgraded our system a couple of weeks ago. They're supposed to make life easier, but that remains to be seen."

Alyx hesitated and for the first time since they'd arrived, she cut a glance at him. He gave her what he hoped was an encouraging smile and she returned a close-lipped one. Her body seemed wound too tight as she sat on the very edge of the chair. "You mentioned boxes?"

"Yes, dear. When your parents passed, we waited the requisite six months for another family member to be located before seeking a permanent foster situation for you. We also took the time to box up all the personal items in your home and put them into storage. Our space is limited, which is why we don't take furniture. I am sorry about that, you had a lovely bedroom set, if I recall."

"Butterflies." The word seemed to pop out of Alyx. "Butterflies and a garden pattern with faux roses and a trellis on the wall. I—I don't know why I said that. I just remembered it."

The description intrigued Daniel. She'd loved his garden from the first day she arrived. It had trellises and roses. He would have to talk to someone about a way to encourage butterflies.

"It's quite all right. We just can't take it all. But the furniture and home would have been sold. Now, the money from those sales would have been put into a fund for your college or for special project needs, if you required it." The woman puffed out a breath. "Hmm, I know we have most of our files transferred now. We began migrating older files to digital a few years ago and this new upgrade meant we should—here." She slid the tablet onto the table and pushed it toward Alyx.

"Your boxes were stored at the Easy-Lock-And-Go on fifteenth. It doesn't show that they were ever picked up, though." The woman's bright smile dimmed, a frown worrying her brow.

"I didn't know they were there."

Daniel pushed away from the wall. "They are still there, aren't they?"

Now the older woman looked stricken and he knew her next words would be disappointing. "After your eighteenth birthday, they would have been held six months, but if they weren't claimed..." She trailed off.

Alyx rubbed her palms against her cheeks and he heard the catch in her voice. "No one told me."

"A letter was sent to your final foster family..." Grace turned the tablet around and read off an address.

"That wasn't my final family. I had to move midterm to a new one... You mean they had all my stuff and a clerical error is why I didn't know it was there?" Anger quavered in the sadness.

"Stay here." The woman squeezed her arm. "I'm going to call down and see if it's still there." But Daniel heard the doubt in her voice, no way Alyx could have missed it. She was twenty-four. They didn't keep the materials past the eighteenth birthday. Six years was too long a stretch of time for hope.

Grace hurried out and Alyx leaned forward, elbow on the table and a hand over her mouth. Daniel pushed the door closed, then moved over to squat next to her, hand braced on the table to keep from touching her. "Hey, don't give up. She remembers you and she wants to help."

"I wish like hell we'd never done this." The earlier anger surged beneath the words. She turned hot eyes on him and he saw the shimmer of tears glazing the surface. "You made me hope for something and I *knew* it was stupid and a bad idea and now..."

She bit off the words and shoved the chair back to stand.

"Let's go."

"We should wait." He held out a placating hand.

She avoided his hand and shook her head. "Don't you get it? Six years ago they sent a letter to an address I was no longer at. They gave me six months to claim my stuff. I never showed up—ergo, I didn't want it. Why would they keep it another six years? There's never enough time or money or space."

Pulling the door open, she spared him a bland look. "I get that you like to solve problems and fix things. You need to learn to accept there are some things you can't fix." She marched away and left him no choice but to follow. He caught up to her as she waved Grace's apology off. "It's okay, Ms. Burrows. I appreciate you looking into it, but you have so much else to do. Don't waste your time on this."

She was out the secure door to the lobby and the tinkle of the bell warned she'd headed outside. Daniel stared after her, then passed over a business card to Ms. Burrows. "Maybe she's right, maybe there's nothing there, but if you find something..."

"I'll contact you, Mr. Voldakov. But you have to understand, I can't release these items to you if I do find them."

"You won't have to. Just get me the message. I'll get her here to pick them up." He left it at that and hit the unlock button on the car remote before stepping outside. Alyx sat in the passenger seat and was belting herself in before he got his side open.

"We have a couple of other opportunities here," he began, but she flattened a palm against the air.

"No. No more digging. This isn't about the past. This is about your business and my 'princessing' it up for you. If we head to the airport now, maybe we can get an earlier flight back."

The conversation ended there. She didn't talk. Didn't press Play on the music. Instead she sat stiff and distant, her gaze away from him, all the way back to the airport. They managed to trade their tickets and boarded a flight less than an hour after leaving the social services office. Each time he tried to touch her arm or her hand, she pulled away from him. She sat as far away from him as the first-class seat would allow, her arms folded and her attitude closed off.

He waited until they were in the air to send some messages via his phone. He told Martin to get the P.I. back on the case. If those boxes were out there, they needed to be found. He also wanted him to scour the news sites and personal social media pages of anyone who may have known the Dagmars.

She might have been too young to have social media account of her own at the time but that didn't mean pictures couldn't have made their way online via old family friends. Her parents had to have had jobs. His people would contact coworkers, former neighbors—anyone who may have a link. When the stewardess came by to offer drinks, Alyx didn't look away from the window.

At LAX, she deplaned ahead of him but maintained a touch-me-not distance that forced his hands to stay in his pockets. By the time they reached his car, his nerves screamed for a return to the camaraderie that marked the beginning of their trip.

The freeze-out remained in place all the way home, where she disappeared into the garden, and he was left to watch her from a distance. By dinner, his teeth and his temper were both on edge. When she picked at her food and refused to look at him, he'd had enough.

"You're pissed and it was a bad day. I get that—"

"Really?" Heat snapped from the words, and she slammed her fork down. "I'm sorry, what foster home did you grow up in? What happened to all of your family valuables? You look like your father, and his father. You *know* your family." The chair fell over as she pushed it back violently and rose. "You hired me to do a job and I'll do it. But you don't know a damn thing about me, rich boy. You haven't lost everything that mattered and become a cog in a wheel of a system that didn't give a damn about you."

"No, but I buried my father when I was a kid." He tossed his napkin on the table. "I grew up in trailer parks and I ran away to video games because it was better than watching my mother try to drink herself to death. We lived paycheck to paycheck when she worked and on my father's pension when she didn't. I wasn't born with a silver spoon in my mouth. Yeah, I'm lucky, I know *exactly* where I came from. I know what failure tastes like and every single thing I have I earned —by busting my ass."

Exhaling hard, he tried to stuff his temper back in the bottle but like the genie it was out. Alyx stared at him and he clenched his hands, counted to ten and let them go again. "No, I don't know what being a foster kid is like and I'm sorrier than you'll ever know that was your childhood. But all I've done is try to help."

"I—" Her voice hitched and a fresh sheen of tears sparkled across her eyes before she turned away. She gripped the back of a chair, and he was torn between going to her and leaving her be.

He kept screwing up with her.

"I'm sorry today sucked for you."

"It pretty much sucked for you too." She sniffled, wheezing a half laugh, half sob.

"I don't know." He raked a hand through his hair to keep from grabbing her like he wanted. "It had waffles."

Her shoulders shook and the last dregs of his anger drained away, leaving a bitter aftertaste in his mouth. Taking a step forward, he started to reach out to her. "Alyx..."

But the face she showed him might have been damp with tears, but also watery laughter. "You're right, it had waffles. I have a bit of a headache. You mind if I go on up?"

Yeah. He minded. But she needed a break. And maybe he did too. "Not at all. Sleep well."

"You too."

Moodily, he stared at the remnants of their

uneaten dinner, then finally headed into his office. Maybe he should do what she asked—butt out of her personal life, keep it all a business transaction.

That way they both got what they wanted. Right?

~

HE WAS asleep on the sofa in his office when a newspaper slapped against his chest. Opening his eyes, he found Victor glaring at him. A hard line knitted the man's brows together. Sitting up slowly, he peered at him. "What's wrong with you?"

"I could ask you the same question, since trouble has erupted in paradise." He pointed to the photo on the front of the social section. Daniel sighed.

It showed Alyx marching away from him and his own confusion mirrored in the grainy photograph. The caption read "Has Spherecast billionaire already crashed and burned his secret romance with 'Russian' princess?"

"Well, shit."

"My thoughts, precisely," Victor scolded. "You have made my job infinitely harder, Mr. Voldakov, and the two of you will have a lot to do to make up lost ground here."

Daniel tossed the paper onto the coffee table and stood. "Leave it alone. We'll take care of it." He should have been paying attention for a photographer. Hell, he'd forgotten about the "job" in his worry for her. She'd shut him out but good.

"No, I will not leave it alone. I warned you that body language would sell or break this plan of yours. After an image like that, after the teases we've leaked for the last week, we're going to have to dig deeper."

"Dig deeper how?" Alyx interrupted from the doorway. Her pale face showed deep smudges beneath her eyes. Had her sleep been as bad as his?

"You'll have to demonstrate the romance to repair this—"

"I can hold her hand, we can dance." Daniel waved away the man's concern, his attention focused on the woman drifting closer. She looked more waiflike than ever before. Her red hair seemed so dark pulled back from her face emphasized the fragility in her features and that damn haunting sadness seemed to have taken up permanent residence in her eyes.

"It will take a lot more than some hand holding." Victor eyed them both. "A great deal more. You should both have breakfast and then brush your teeth."

Alyx swung her gaze away from him to stare at Victor in confusion. "Our teeth?"

"Yes, your teeth. You'll be kissing today, and a lot of it, until you make me believe that you two can't think of anything else. Then you'll go out tonight and show the world just how much you want each other."

Daniel froze.

Oh shit, indeed.

CHAPTER 14
ALYX

True to his word, Victor gave them time to eat breakfast, drink coffee and brush their teeth before he locked all three of them up in the study.

Alyx buried the disappointment of the day before—or tried to, at least. She wasn't sure she wanted to keep up with this charade. They were what? Just a couple of weeks in and her soul was raw and shredded. What would she be like two months?

"All right. We're going to pretend that you're both amateurs at this." Victor carried his coffee cup over to a side table and set it down. He drew out a tin of peppermints from his jacket pocket, then placed them on the coffee table. "Every kiss tells a story."

Perching on the edge of the sofa, she chose the spot farthest from where Daniel stood. No matter how rationally she reminded herself that the loss of all those personal items was hardly his fault, the hope to have them again was. He'd insisted on the trip. He drove her from the parking lot where her house used to be to social services and he got the ball rolling.

In all honesty, she was no worse off than she'd been before they went. She didn't have any personal belongings outside of her bear. But she'd never known she missed that chance before.

Never knew that a clerical error sent the letter to the wrong address. Never knew she should have asked about it.

So why does it hurt to look at him?

"Princess." Victor snapped her back to the present and she met his stern gaze while trying to stuff all that hope-deflated disappointment back into the Pandora's box they'd inadvertently opened.

"Yes?"

"Are you listening?" He knew she wasn't or he wouldn't have called her on it.

Sighing, she crossed one leg over the other and folded her arms before sitting back against the sofa. "No. Not really."

"Okay. You need to get your head in this game. I'm not going to ask what happened yesterday. It doesn't matter. Do you remember the role you're taking on?"

This time she really *looked* at Daniel. Exhaustion left dark circles beneath his eyes. His tousled blond hair and hint of stubble on his cheeks gave his normally good-boy, sun-kissed looks a rakish edge. The corners of his mouth turned up in a small smile. Her heart thudded a little harder.

"Yes. I am his soon-to-be fiancée, and princess, or grand duchess, as is the proper title."

"Excellent. And you, Mr. Voldakov? You do remember the part you play in your own masquerade?" Victor's tone took a harder edge with Daniel, his words clipping off on the last syllable.

The photo was bad, she knew that—but that hadn't been Daniel's fault. It was hers.

"Victor, I appreciate the candor and the lessons, but don't push too much harder." The mild warning was the first she'd ever heard Daniel make and her thighs tightened at the tense quality of his voice.

"Good. You need to remember that in this situation you are the man. You take the lead. You set the tone." Their coach seemed oblivious to the tension winding in the air, or maybe he just chose to ignore it. "Selling a romance requires understanding what that romance is— what the body language communicates. Kissing is a vital component to the whole package. You were doing very well with your touching. You brushed legs while sharing meals, you held hands and you sat close together. But yesterday's events have now illuminated a schism... which is being repeated in this room right now."

He looked meaningfully at the space between her and Daniel. Alyx sighed and stood as Daniel took two steps forward. She bumped into him and he slung an arm around her waist, steadying her. Her heart pounded hard against her ribs, but he didn't let her go. "Is this really necessary?"

She hadn't meant to ask the question. After all this was a job. Only a job.

If nothing else, the explosion the night before drove that point home. Maybe if she repeated that to herself as a mantra, she'd make it clear to her out-of-whack emotions that they weren't personally invested in this. She was still Alyx Dagmar, aspiring actress, and this was the opportunity of a lifetime.

Why were her nerves tingling and her stomach upset? He couldn't possibly be a bad kisser and she'd already thought about what it would be like to—

Disaster lay down that track.

"That's a fair question." Oh, thank God. Daniel was on her side in this. He stared at Victor. "We don't really need you to walk us through the kissing. I'm pretty sure we both understand how that works."

"Well, then by all means, demonstrate." Victor stared at them expectantly and her hopes dashed against the cold practicality of the situation. They couldn't hope to sell a romance without passion.

Why did I agree to this?

She looked up at Daniel, half expecting to see her worried emotions reflected in his gaze, but what she found startled her more. Interest gleamed in his eyes. Intrigue and maybe a note of longing. All the moisture fled her mouth. He lifted his free hand and brushed a tendril of hair back from her face.

Every muscle in her body seized. Electricity

skated across her cheek at the casual touch of his fingers. Her heart squeezed, pulsing in little beats as though afraid to interrupt. His head tilted and all she could see were his blue eyes staring into hers as he swooped in. At the last moment, her lashes fluttered closed and his breath tickled her lips, a promise of the moment when they would touch.

"No." That single word interrupted the moment and Daniel jerked against her. Eyes flying open, she swung a look at Victor. "Your body language is wrong."

"I thought we were kissing." Frustration cracked a note in her voice and she grimaced at Daniel's low chuckle.

"We were almost kissing, but apparently we needed to have some cut scenes for the blooper reel." Daniel squeezed her lightly.

The wildly inappropriate remark sent a titter of amusement through her and she snickered. Victor frowned and the deeper his frown went, the more humor escaped. She turned her face toward Daniel's shoulder and leaned into him—shaking with suppressed laughter.

He rubbed her back, his own chest reverberating with the hilarity of the situation. Glancing up, her nose bumped his and he kissed her.

Victor be damned on whether they were doing it right, but her smile faded as his lips caressed hers, the barest hint of contact—completely ruined when she leaned into it and their noses bumped.

Laughter erupted again.

Daniel caught her as she sagged against him, both fumbling until they ended up sitting on the sofa.

"Again."

She barely had time to process the word when Daniel's open mouth met hers and their teeth clacked. It was her turn to withdraw and she covered her mouth with a hand, embarrassment flooding through her. "I really do know how to do this," she said from behind her fingers.

"I've got some experience myself, not that you can tell at the moment." His self-deprecating humor set her free and the giggles spilled out. She leaned away, but her leg still rested against his. She couldn't stop the silly sounds from escaping. Tears gathered in the corners of her eyes and she spared a look at Victor.

That was a mistake. His disapproving scowl sent another wave of humor through her and she collapsed back against the sofa and drew her knees to her chest. Daniel stared down at her, his own grin widening. "Okay, maybe we do need lessons."

"Maybe." She rubbed at the corners of her eyes, trying to get a grip.

He winked at her, then canted a look at Victor. "Want to tell us what we're doing wrong?"

"In general or specifically?" The arid tone tickled her further and she hiccuped a choked laugh. "The humor is good. You're both relaxing. The second kiss was better than the first but the third was just dreadful."

"What was wrong with the first kiss?" Alyx

sat up abruptly. She'd actually been looking forward to that one. Daniel caught her hand and she curled her fingers around his.

"He pursued you, but you just stood there, waiting for it to happen—terrified." As quiet as his voice was, Victor's tone rang with judgment.

"I wasn't terrified." Not exactly. "I was nervous. We've never kissed before."

"Precisely my point." Victor rose and held out a hand to her imperiously. She sneaked a look at Daniel and he shook his head slightly. He didn't know what the coach planned to throw at them next.

Accepting Victor's hand, she let him pull her to her feet and away from the sofa. Unfortunately, that meant letting go of Daniel. Victor led her into the center of the room and set a hand on her hip. If he hadn't been correcting her posture and stance for the past several days, she might have slapped his hand—as it was, she obeyed his directions. He slid an arm around her.

"When Mr. Voldakov went to kiss you earlier, this is how you stood—he had the control and the lead, but you were neither inviting nor seeking. You merely stood." Victor lowered his face toward hers and unlike with Daniel her lashes didn't flutter nor did her heart pick up speed. "Not even when you could feel his breath on your lips did you reach out to touch him. He caressed your face, he sought an invitation and *still* you didn't move."

As if to illustrate his point, he touched her cheek and closed the final gap to touch his lips to hers. It was a cool, almost impersonal peck and felt about fifty shades of wrong. She caught her lower lip in her teeth as he drew back. From the corner of her eye, she caught sight of the look on Daniel's face—a scowl that could have mirrored Victor's earlier frown.

"When you want a man to kiss a woman, she has to let him know the overture is not only welcome, but demanded." Victor instructed, picking up her hand and putting it on his shoulder. He glanced meaningfully at her feet. "She takes a step forward, into the man."

Reluctantly, she slid her foot forward and that left her off balance until she practically leaned on Victor, draping into his arms, and he was the only thing standing between her and falling on her ass.

"Now smile, just a hint of one, and you look at his mouth, or his eyes, but you watch as he swoops in. Just before he arrives, you lift up onto your toes and meet him—offering both invitation and demand." Victor dipped his head and watched her expectantly. Did he really want her to kiss him?

A cough interrupted. "I think we have it now."

She tossed a grateful look at Daniel and stepped back, regaining her balance. He held out his hand and she took it. Daniel tugged her to his side of the study and glanced down at her. "Just forget the coach over there."

His jaw tightened with a tension she hadn't seen there before. He gave Victor a hard, territorial look. "And no comments from the gallery. If you want us to get this right, you let us do it our way."

Victor spread his arms and retreated a few steps.

Heart thumping, she fought another wild grin as Daniel slid his arm around her waist. A glint of humor twinkled in his eyes and her grin grew. "We're going to clack teeth again," she warned him.

"No. We're not." He brushed his fingers down her cheek and her pulse leaped.

She slid her hand up his shirt to his shoulder, the fabric warm and soft against the taut muscle beneath. Her stomach clenched. "We're going to bump noses."

"No. We're not." A hint of a smile creased his lips as he gave her a light tug and she slid her foot forward, gliding into him until her breasts pushed up against his chest. Her body sizzled at the contact.

He dipped his head, his blue gaze holding her captive. She couldn't think of a single objection and remembered to push up on her toes as his lips settled against hers. Her fingers closed on his shirt, fisting the fabric, and her mind soared. His mouth worked magic, massaging her lips apart, and when his tongue glided against hers, a wild-fire raced through her blood. He made a low sound in his throat and his arm tightened on her waist. Somewhere between the first brush of his lips and his tongue gliding over hers, she threaded her fingers into his hair.

The masculine scent of him filled her nostrils and a curl of liquid heat skated from her nipples to her sex.

Good God, the man can kiss.

When his palm smoothed over the curve of her ass, she pulled back, startled. She stared at him, breathing ragged, her thoughts a wild cacophony of regret and longing.

"Much better." Victor's voice intruded and she withdrew further, aware of the branding hand shaping her bottom and the fingers curling into the back pocket of her jeans. He wasn't going to let her go. That light, possessive touch burned through the denim.

Now what? she wanted to ask, but the words wouldn't quite come out.

"And again," Victor instructed, resuming his seat in the chair.

Her gaze flew up to meet Daniel's and she saw the promise in them as he tugged her closer and her fingers slid back into his hair. He fit against her, perfectly, and her breath caught just before his lips touched hers. Knowing what to expect didn't prepare her for the explosions rioting in her senses.

Just a kiss. Just a kiss.

But she couldn't disguise the small moan that slid out nor miss the throaty masculine murmur of sound that matched it.

It was a hell of a lot more than just a kiss.

CHAPTER 15
DANIEL

They made their debut splash as a public couple at a small event raising money for Malibu Beach recovery before advancing to several charity events over the next week.

The photographers, having sensed blood in the water with the initial social page, followed them. It took everything in Daniel to keep the act up, particularly when all he wanted to do when he kissed her was pull her away somewhere quiet and explore just how far those kisses could take him. It was an exercise in pure sensual torture. If not for her insistence on sleeping on the sofa, he had a feeling they might have already taken it past their agreement.

"It's working." Martin sailed into Daniel's office. Daniel glanced up from loading his briefcase. He'd just signed all of the outstanding papers Lucy'd collected for him. Amazingly, his secretary wasn't ready to hang him after his conspicuous absences and constant working from home. If he wasn't reviewing code, he was out with Alyx—holding her hand, kissing her plump, sweet lips and driving himself slowly insane.

"What's working?" The thick vellum invitation was the one they'd been waiting for. Local problems in Japan delayed the CEO's visit to Los Angeles, but he was scheduled to arrive Friday. The company had planned a large charity event to help promote recovery in both of their respective areas.

"You and Her Royal Hotness." Martin slid a paper across to him. "I just got the heads-up that this is running in tomorrow's Journal. It's already live on their site and *People* magazine just put in a call. They want to meet with the Princess Alyxandretta and hear her story."

The single sheet of paper included the Journal's letterhead and a byline from one of their most popular gossip columnists, a woman renowned for scoring interviews with the most reluctant of celebrities. He gave the release a cursory glance.

Spherecast billionaire and his "royal" girlfriend showed some PDA while taking a stroll on day three of the Coachella Music Festival in Indio, California. The cute couple shared a kiss as they enjoyed their time together watching indie band Fever take the stage alongside such notable film actors as Diana Keegan and Josh Jamison. Networking opportunities for the aspiring actress?

The day before, the two were spotted attending a pool party at the Beverly Hilton and later headed down to Santa Monica for another PDA-filled ride on the Ferris wheel. Royal watchers are turning their eyes to the mysterious princess and the blossoming love affair.

Sources close to the couple have identified the princess's interest in film and stage roles. In the fun column, the billionaire apparently staged an elaborate audition to get a first date. What show would you like to see the princess appear on?

"It's working. I've had some feelers from the grand duke. Cursory calls from the local law firm that represents his interests and an inquiry about your schedule." Martin looked ready to burst with smugness.

"Great." He tossed the sheet in with the rest in his briefcase and closed it. "Anything else?"

"No." Martin slid his hands into his pockets. "Heading out already? It's barely three."

"Was just a drop by to sign some things for Lucy. We're driving to Napa this evening to attend a party." He hit the button on his desk. "Lucy, did my tux come back from the cleaners?"

"Of course it did and I already sent it to the house. It will be waiting for you. Miss Dagmar called. She said to let you know she would be about an hour late."

"Is everything all right?" He ignored Martin's smirk.

"Yes, sir. Apparently, there was a shoe emergency. Something to do with the dress she is wearing." Lucy didn't bother to contain her amusement. "She had to make some calls to find the pair she wanted, but now she's stuck in traffic."

Stuck in traffic? Her car couldn't handle heavy

traffic and if he knew Alyx—which he did rather well by now—she'd probably taken her own vehicle rather than the driver he arranged for her.

"Do me a favor? Call her back and see where she is stuck and if you can help her out?" He cut a glance to his watch. If he left now, he could pick up the orchids from the florist rather than waiting on their delivery. The Chanel evening gala was his least favorite event, but when they'd gone over the social schedule with Victor, he hadn't missed the light leaping into her eyes so he'd agreed to it. The corsage was old-fashioned, but a popular accessory for the attendees to wear along with their evening finery.

"Absolutely. Now you need to go. You still have a haircut appointment." Lucy clicked off the intercom and Daniel swore. He'd forgotten about the haircut. But if Alyx ran late that still gave him some time. Scooping up his case, he swung around the desk and headed for the door.

"Racquetball this weekend?" Martin called after him.

"Can't." Daniel waved to Lucy and glanced at Martin as he followed him to the elevator. "We'll be in Napa until Sunday evening. Maybe next week."

The elevator doors whooshed closed, cutting off whatever response Martin may have made.

∼

ALYX

It was a cool evening and the air carried a wild variety of spicy scents from grapes to the hint of coffee, sage, rosemary...and something more elusive that she couldn't quite identify. The heels she wore were magnificently comfortable and perfectly silver, a smashing complement to the skin-baring Grecian wrap. The silver metallic knot strap and drape floated around her. She'd picked the color because it reminded her of Daniel's eyes, and the look on his face when he saw her filled her with a lush sense of accomplishment.

He'd presented her with the most elegant single-orchid corsage she'd ever seen. As he'd slipped the strap over her wrist, she'd been transported back to prom, that annual hell event for seniors. Especially seniors like her who didn't have a date or know most of the kids attending. She'd gone anyway, had her picture taken and danced. But no good-looking jock or lean-built nerd had given her a corsage.

Until tonight.

Arm in arm, they strolled through the candlelit vineyards, pausing to chat with the others, mingling among the guests. But Alyx didn't really pay much attention to the names or the faces. Daniel's arm was warm against her and he kept lifting her fingers to his lips, the butterfly kisses turning her insides to jelly. When the music started and he swept her into a dance, she forgot about the rest of the party and the role she was supposed to be playing.

"What's going on in that mind of yours?"

Shivers raced through her as his lips brushed against her ear. She closed her eyes. It was easy to just get lost in this story they'd created.

"I was thinking I feel like a princess tonight. And not because of the dress or the shoes or the atmosphere." She leaned back, looking at him as he turned her away from the other guests. The comforting weight of his arms around her and the singular focus of his gaze locked on her combined to transport her to a magical spot where the party, the guests—hell the world—all faded away.

"You are a princess, sweetheart." He dipped down and stole a kiss—a casual, easy brush of his lips to hers, igniting that sensual ache crying out inside.

"No, not that kind of princess." She licked her lips, enjoying the hint of his taste that lingered there. "It's hard to explain."

"Try." The music shifted to a more popular love song and the band apparently had a singer, because his low baritone crooned out the words.

"I told you about going to my high school prom." That confession came over a pair of banana splits and a *Red Dwarf* marathon he'd surprised her with late one night. She'd never met anyone who liked the old British science fiction show the way she did.

"Yep, I remember." His fingers stroked her

back, light little touches that reminded her he was there—as if she could forget.

"I didn't have a date."

"Because high school boys are stupid." He didn't miss a beat and she couldn't help but laugh.

"Well, maybe, but in their defense, I was the new girl. It's hard to be the new girl at the big blowout to celebrate the end of your high school career." Once upon a time that hurt, but she'd moved past it. "I went to the prom, I bought a dress, I got shoes, I dressed up and I danced. I danced with girls, I danced with guys, I danced by myself. I got my picture taken."

"And this?" He nodded to the swaying lanterns casting their muted romantic glows and the luxuriously attired couples dancing around them. "It reminds you of prom?"

"Oh no. It's about a thousand times better than prom." She grinned. "Not only do I have a dress and shoes—" she leaned in conspiratorially, "—I have the best-looking date here and he gave me a corsage."

"Lucky, lucky man." He matched her smile and tugged her closer, fisting her joined hands against his chest. His mouth slanted over hers and she was lost in the gentle massage of his tongue seeking entrance, the pounding of his heart and the feel of his palm gliding across her lower back, just skimming the curve of her hip.

The telltale whir of a camera and the eye-blinding flash pulled them out of their haze and she blinked slowly. Daniel gave the man a mild look of irritation, but the photographer ignored them, moving on to take another picture.

"You want to get out of here?" he murmured.

Her heart squeezed. "Yes...but I'd like to dance one more song."

"Whatever you want."

~

Daniel

AN HOUR LATER, they wandered through the vineyard back toward the house they were staying in. His hosts had waved them off when they paused at their table to give their excuses. He slipped off his suit jacket and draped it around her shoulders when a chilly breeze swept through the grapes.

"Thank you for bringing me to this one." The moonlight emphasized the graceful column of her neck when she glanced up at him.

"It was an excellent choice."

"And you do business with none of those people." She danced ahead of him, stretching his arm out as she twirled and faced him, walking backward. "They're fashion designers, wine-makers, directors, movie producers and celebrities."

He laughed softly and shook his head. "No, I don't do business with any of them. It's rather remarkable that we were invited, wasn't it?" Victor'd pointed out that this invitation was the first of many, a tacit acknowledgment of Alyx's status and something they should take advantage of. If she hadn't gotten excited about the location, he wouldn't have cared one way or the other.

Better to not examine his motivations with regard to that.

"Thank you." She waggled her brows playfully. "It's beautiful here and I had a lot of fun."

"Me too." Strangely enough, he really had enjoyed it. From the wine tour they took the first day to the tasting they'd attended the night before, to this morning's tennis doubles with their hosts and a handful of other guests. Alyx never failed to surprise him, least of all with her ability to hit the ball on the courts.

He hadn't realized she knew how to play tennis.

"Good." At the edge of the vineyard, they crossed over onto a well-manicured lawn with decadently thick grass. The lack of rain in the region hadn't stopped their hosts from using judicious irrigation to keep the area green and beautiful. Alyx paused to slip off her shoes, bracing one hand on his arm for support.

Wiggling her toes in the grass she grinned. "Okay, they didn't hurt earlier, but my pinkie toes are not happy with me."

The absolute lack of guile and artlessness she delivered with the line was just one of the many reasons he enjoyed her. *I adore her. She's wonderful.* The thought crept out to ambush him. But he couldn't dispute the validity of the sentiment.

She paused on the steps and glanced at him. "Daniel?"

"Hmm?" He tucked the emotions away for examination later.

"You okay?" Concern edged around her quiet joy.

"Great. I was just thinking we're going to have a hard time secreting our ice cream upstairs." It was the first thought that crossed his mind and when her eyes lit up, he was glad for it. "Tell you what. Head up and get changed. I'll see what I can do."

"Okay." She skipped ahead of him and he blew out a long breath. It was hard to take his gaze off her. Shaking off the stupor, he diverted from the stairs to head into the kitchen. The cook took almost no bribing to prepare the hot fudge sundaes with nuts. He carried both up the stairs along with a carafe of hot coffee and two mugs.

Their shared guest room was empty, but a light shone under the en suite bathroom door. "I'm almost done," she called.

"Take your time but the ice cream might melt."

Her little whoop at the comment brought another smile to his lips. He stripped off the rest of his suit and left the cufflinks on the dresser. By the time the bathroom door opened and she appeared, face scrubbed and a hairbrush in hand, he was settled on the bed in a pair of loose shorts and a T-shirt. She grinned at the tray he'd set on the nightstand and slid up onto the comforter next to him.

Unfortunately, the guest room didn't boast a sofa and rather than let her take the floor, where she'd most certainly tried to sleep their first night in, he'd taken the bullet and ordered her onto the bed. He'd certainly slept worse places and thankfully, she'd let him have the win.

"Do you think we're too late for tonight's marathon?" She set the hairbrush aside and claimed her sundae.

"Nope." Daniel grinned and pointed at the television, paused on the opening credits to the science fiction show.

"Yes!" She made a little fist pump with her spoon and they toasted with their sundae glasses. As soon as she curled her legs up and propped a pillow across her lap, he killed the lights and hit Play.

Three episodes later, they'd devoured their sundaes, finished the coffee and she curled against his side.

Sound asleep.

He stroked a finger across her hair and shifted a little to make her more comfortable, but when she just burrowed closer he leaned back against the headboard with a sigh. The first time he actually had her in a bed and he was going to sleep sitting up.

Her fingers wrapped into his T-shirt and he smiled.

There were worse things.

CHAPTER 16
ALYX

Twin bands of hot steel held her tight and secure. She stretched slowly. The pillow beneath her head shifted and a warm hand closed on her breast.

Awareness jolted through her sleep-fogged mind. Her eyes flew open to face the wall of their guest room at the Hamilton house—the Napa Valley estate where they stayed. She lay on her side, pillowed against Daniel's shoulder. His body pressed up against hers, wrapping her up, and his hand had possession of her breast. The thin T-shirt she slept in was hardly a barrier and her nipple pebbled against his palm.

When he squeezed, his thumb rolling over the hardened tip, she had to swallow back a groan. His erection tucked against her bottom, long and stiff.

Two disparate desires collided. She needed to extricate herself from his arms and that was the sensible choice. But when he shifted, turning onto his back and pulling her around to face him,

179

the urge to stay right there and explore the passion his kisses filled her with overrode good sense.

He massaged her breast and slid his other hand down her hip. When his fingers splayed against the waistband of her shorts, she made a little noise. His body stilled against her and she twisted, her gaze colliding with his sleepy, long-lashed eyes.

Get up and move away. The sober advice chirped into her mind as though delivered by Jiminy Cricket. Dropping her gaze to his lips, she licked her own and his hand glided up her back to catch the back of her neck.

Move away, she reminded herself sternly, but she didn't listen. His gaze was like a caress on her face, his body, lean and hot where it pressed into hers. He held her captive as he stroked his thumb across the nipple, teasing it through her T-shirt, and she lunged into him, meeting his mouth for a kiss that burned through her barriers.

His tongue teased the seam of her lips and she opened for him. Excitement thrilled to every nerve ending as he stroked her hair and down the line of her back. Somehow she sprawled across him, almost grinding against the rigid length of his cock. The kiss broke for a hesitant second. Alertness filled his blue eyes. Alertness, and something far more decadent.

Want.

"Alyx." His husky voice wrapped around her name and she sighed, a ribbon of need tightening in her belly. He stared up at her as his hand left her neck, slid down her spine and dipped below the edge of her shorts. The contact sizzled where his fingertips stroked her skin.

"This is a bad idea." She breathed the words, fighting the urge to squirm, because movement reminded her of their precarious position.

But her body hummed with every light caress. He palmed her breast, petting it in a slow circular fashion that just ratcheted up the need boiling inside her.

"It doesn't have to be." He lifted his head, catching her lower lip in a sucking kiss as he traced the line of her bottom. Flesh against flesh and she wanted more. Her knees clamped on his hips and she tried to push herself up.

The slow motion only served to intensify the heat between her thighs, the rigid throb of his erection teasing her through their clothes. She knew he took care of his body. She'd seen the hard plane of his stomach, the golden smoothness of his shoulders, the fine—almost baby-fine —sprinkle of hair that circled his nipples.

Arched above him, she savored how his hand slipped down to the hem of her shirt. Even the most casual graze against her firing her nerves. It was time to stop. They were both awake. Both aware.

But he pushed her shirt up, then his hand caught her breast, his thumb and forefinger rolled her nipple. She tipped her head back. Raw desire pulsed through her, igniting a liquid heat in her blood that threatened to boil over. He pushed her shirt higher and she watched him staring at her. He studied her breasts, and it took everything she had not to sit up straighter, arch her back and offer them to him.

Thank God he didn't need the offer. One moment she straddled him and the next she lay on her back, legs wrapped around his hips as his golden head dropped to her chest. His breath warmed one nipple. Her sex clenched and she thrust her fingers into his hair.

All thoughts of pushing him away evaporated.

"I want you." His murmured words echoed her own thoughts and then his lips closed over one aching, turgid peak and she gave up any pretense. Her back arched, thrusting the bud into his mouth, and he grazed the sensitive tip with his teeth before latching on to it in a hard suck that pulled all that aching, wanton need to the forefront. His hips ground to hers, teasing her through their clothes with a mock thrust. She stroked her nails down his back, found the hem of his shirt and glided them back up the warm heat of his skin.

Electricity pumped through her, like summer lightning rippling through her body. Somewhere between the first touch of his lips to her nipple and his wet kisses tracing a path to the other, her shirt hit the floor and so did his. He surged up and caught her mouth in a kiss that demanded as much as he gave. The light hairs on his chest tickled her breasts and she hitched her legs higher, wrapping them around him. His tongue stroked hers, swirling, teasing and tasting. The hot, rich spicy scent of his masculinity filled her, imprinting on her soul. When he slid his hand beneath her waistband, she held her breath.

He lifted his head as two of his fingers glided along the damp seam of her pussy and she didn't even try to suppress the moan. A possessive smile lifted the corners of his mouth and his blue, blue eyes darkened.

"You are so wet," he whispered. The raw declaration sent another flood of heat through her and she pushed her hips up, grinding against those fingers exploring her folds. He cupped her pussy in his palm and began a slow back-and-forth glide against her clit.

Weeks of drugging kisses, casual touches and wonderful company left her primed for the wildness threading through her. She fisted a hand into his hair and dragged him upward, and he caught her mouth in another kiss as a finger slid inside her. She bucked against his hand, wanting —no, needing—more. Her body hummed, her heart shattering the restrictive bands she'd encircled it with.

He drove her higher, thrusting her over the peak, and pleasure exploded through her. She drifted on the eddies of the pleasure he'd given her and she ran her hands up and down his back. She wanted more. She wanted him inside her, filling her, and she rode his hand with a demand of her own.

Petting her through the orgasm, his kisses grew less feverish. He teased her, nibbling at her lips and tracing a path to her ear. When he latched on to her earlobe, a fresh wave of tension coiled through her. "Daniel..." she exhaled on a whisper, barely able to contain the emotions boiling up inside her.

"Shh," he soothed, his breath warm as he traced his tongue around the whorls of her ear. His hands continued to pet, to stroke, and when she caught fire again, he caught her clit between his thumb and forefinger. The barest of pressure and she imploded all over again, her head arching back, and he covered her mouth with his to swallow her cries of pleasure.

Cool air rushed against her breasts, tightening her nipples. She opened her eyes to find him sitting. He dragged her shorts and panties down and tossed them off the edge of the bed. His own shorts slid off his hips and she lifted up on an elbow, drinking in the glorious sight of him.

His cock jutted, thick and full. He reached across her to the nightstand and she dragged her fingers down his chest. She wanted to touch him. Bad idea or not, she didn't know and frankly, she no longer cared. His muscles jerked and jumped with every touch and he fumbled with a curse. His wallet slid off the bed and she slithered along him as he chased it. She bit down on his shoulder, his hot skin salty with a gleam of sweat. She found his nipple and swirled her tongue around it, remembering what he did to her.

A low groan vibrated through his chest. "You're killing me." He laughed, but he didn't pull away as he came up with his wallet. She barely noticed the tinfoil in his hand as she taste-tested her way across his chest. His abdominal muscles rippled and she inched lower. One tentative touch of her mouth to his erection and he jerked, pulling away and lunging up to catch her hands.

"You do that and I will come in about thirty seconds," he warned, his face tight. A vein throbbed in his forehead and his blue eyes were dark with a need she understood only too well.

"You say that like it's a bad thing," she teased, stroking the hard length of him with her palm from balls to tip and back. He hissed out a breath and buried his face against her neck. He bit her, the lightest grazing of his teeth, then he sucked at her skin and a fresh riot of sensations broke out over her.

"It is when I want to come inside you." The rawness undid her. The strength of his touch, the naked vulnerability in his words and the passion in his eyes seduced her objections. She lifted her hands in surrender, tipping her chin back and thrusting her breasts toward him.

"Thirty seconds," she advised, a playful grin tipping her lips. "And then all bets are off."

Her heart hiccupped as his full lips turned in another devastating grin. He ripped the foil on the package and she watched as he rolled the condom into place. The ache between her thighs became a demanding pulse. She was hardly a virgin or inexperienced and at the same time, she wasn't sure she'd ever wanted someone as much as she wanted him.

Drinking in the sight of him, she scraped her teeth over her lower lip even as she savored how gorgeous he was. She wanted to touch him. She wanted to skate her fingers over every muscle, explore every twitch, drown in the contact of his skin against hers. All the reasons they shouldn't do this evaporated.

The words "no sex clause" whispered against the back of her mind, a taunt? A tease? Or just a reminder? Dragging her gaze back up to Daniel's, Alyx forgot how to breathe. The clause made sense when she didn't know him.

That was then... Right? We don't need that anymore, do we?

"Alyx," he exhaled her name like a caress. The look in his eyes shredded what was left of her reservations. This was Daniel.

"I'm here," she promised, cupping his cheek in her palm. The warmth of his skin reminded her that they were wrapped up in each other. The stubble decorating his jaw prickled at her palm. Reality and fantasy twining together.

"Any second thoughts?" He searched her face. "If you have them..."

She pressed her fingers to his lips, understanding what he wasn't saying. "No," she said, whispering in the same hushed tone he used. "I have no second thoughts, not right now. I want this...I want you."

It was true. She didn't. Maybe that wasn't the best idea or even a good idea, but she didn't want to focus on any of that. She just wanted to be with him.

He closed his eyes briefly. "Thank fuck." Then he tumbled her onto her back. As he settled between her thighs, he kept his gaze locked on hers. It left her bare, open, and utterly exposed. The way the muscle in his jaw ticked as though it was taking every ounce of his control.

Fire burned in those stunning blue eyes, fire and something more. Something she'd never seen in anyone else's eyes before. It buffeted her in a way she couldn't explain and didn't want to at the moment,

As he slid into her, she fisted his hair. The tension winding tighter and tighter within her left her shaking. As his cock stretched inch by inch, a laugh escaped. It wasn't just the raw, unvarnished emotion from him but a heady inescapable one from herself. She twined her legs around his hips and tugged his head down.

He thrust into her, stretching her as their mouths collided. Locked in a duel of tongues, he drove into her over and over. She raced her hands rom his hair to his ass, then dug her nails into those taut cheeks that flexed with every surge.

"You feel so good," she admitted in between deep, biting kisses and his huff made her laugh again. The sounds just had her inner muscles clamping and his breath hissed out as he tightened his arms around her.

They came together, over and over, when he rolled onto his back, she arched above him. It took little encouragement to get her to roll her hips as she rode him. She was torn between just sinking into the motions and watching him as he gazed up at her.

Need and desire eddied up, and she stretched to the point of breaking. Between his thrusts and her hips rolling, she hit her clit with just the right amount of pressure that her vision blurring.

"Right there," she gasped out and dug her fingers into his shoulders.

"I have you," he said, tumbling with her again. She was sure there were more words, but she didn't hear them as she came apart and his shout followed her.

～

DANIEL

They collapsed together, tumbling as he chased her pleasure with his own. The feel of her muscles trembling and the squeeze of her around his cock was so goddamn decadent, he wanted to repeat it immediately. Even after their release, they clung together, skin sticky with sweat and heat.

She wasn't the only one trembling. His mind pitched between stirring to kiss her again and just lying there, savoring the warmth of her body nestled against his. They'd certainly violated the no-sex clause. That thought and that thought alone nudged him into action.

He shifted, peeling himself upward. Her eyes opened, revealing lazy pleasure, and he gave in to the temptation of her plump lips, swollen from his kisses, to taste her again. She slid warm arms around him and nuzzled his lips, soft, open and willing to his invasion.

Need thrummed through him and his cock twitched. They were going to need another condom. A box of condoms. He would invest in a damn condom company. He traced the liquid kisses across her cheek and nibbled at her earlobe. The soft flesh tasted sweet—the delicate, feminine citrusy scent of her filled his nostrils. He inhaled a long, drugging hit of it and sighed against her.

So many things he wanted to do to her—and with her. A knock on the door rapped reality back into their sensual interlude and he lifted his head, glaring at the door. "What?"

Her body clenched around him and his gaze swooped down to her suppressed giggles. The desire in her eyes lightened to amusement and he couldn't help but grin.

"Mr. Voldakov—Miss Dagmar—" He heard a man clearing his throat. "Breakfast is served in the atrium."

Daniel groaned. She nibbled his throat.

The man at their door coughed lightly. "Please pardon the intrusion, but the presentation will begin in a few minutes."

Presentation.

Breakfast.

Their Napa Valley hosts.

He just didn't give a damn.

Her voice was a throaty whisper in his ear.

"We go home tonight. We can afford to go down and be seen."

He grimaced. He had no desire to leave this room or this bed in the foreseeable future. A shuffling sound in the hallway warned him that the man waited for a response.

"We will be along shortly," he grumbled. He scowled and at Alyx's arched brows, he tacked on, "Thank you."

"Very good, sir. Thank you both." The man at the door left, and Daniel decided to ignore him. He wanted to play with her breasts and see how many licks it took to get her to gasp again, but she gave him a little push.

"No, no. We have to go down, remember."

"I would be happy to go down on you." He grinned and she rewarded him with another throaty laugh. She kissed his chin, his cheek, and then the corner of his mouth. He slanted his head, taking the kiss and drawing on her tongue as she darted it against his. Her nails glided down his spine and his cock twitched again. Just a few more minutes and he'd be more than ready. But her nails were sharp when she pinched his ass and he lifted his head to find her amused gaze, albeit fogged with desire, staring up at him.

"We have to shower and get dressed." But her smile held the promise of more.

"I don't want to." It was probably the single most petulant thing he'd ever said, but she was already wiggling out of his arms. As she slid off the edge of the bed, he felt bereft.

"I know, but we go home after the presentation. Depending on how fast you drive, we could make it in time for a long—long nap." Her saucy little wink eased the disappointment at having to get up. She sashayed to the bathroom, completely unabashed at her nudity. At the door, she glanced back. "Aren't you coming?"

His brows rose as he removed the condom and tied it off.

"They seemed to be in a hurry. We could save time and water if we showered together."

The disappointment ballooning in his gut punctured with a fresh wave of heat. He lunged off the bed, dropping the used condom in the trash and snagging another foil package off the nightstand before he caught her. Picking her up, he carried her into the shower and pressed her against the cool tile, mouth fixing against hers. Somewhere between kissing her and soaping her breasts, she wiggled an escape and teased his cock back to full life.

They were late for breakfast.

Daniel didn't give a damn.

CHAPTER 17
ALYX

Han Takahashi was an absolute gentleman, but he definitely wasn't comfortable with dancing. Alyx held herself loosely in his arms as they waltzed around the floor. The private party took place in the executive suites of the Takahashi building. Over his shoulder she caught sight of Daniel and smiled. He grinned, leaning against the bar, surrounded by the company's executives, and his gaze never left hers.

"Thank you for the dance, Your Highness." Takahashi's words jerked her attention back, which was probably a good thing. She and Daniel had barely come up for air since returning from Napa. He'd canceled appointments, preferring to stay in bed. She'd discovered that he could debug his programs naked—an issue apparently when she completely distracted him.

They were like a pair of randy teenagers, barely able to keep their hands off each other.

The balloon of lust floated them higher and higher.

But tonight's dinner party was unavoidable. The CEO of the Takahashi Corporation flew all the way to Los Angeles just to meet with Daniel and to thank him personally for Spherecast's assistance in recovering so many of their files. Those meetings meant she'd barely seen Daniel all day, but she could feel his gaze sliding over her with every turn around the dance floor—caressing her skin, teasing her senses.

The music ended and Takahashi released her. He offered her the most formal of bows and she returned it, perfectly. *Thank you, Victor, for that lesson.*

A hand glided up her spine as the music began again. Daniel smiled at the CEO. "If you will allow me a few moments, Mr. Takahashi, I'll join you and your board for drinks after."

"Of course." Takahashi bowed again and Daniel tugged her into his arms. She fit against him, and the room's occupants faded as they danced.

"He really likes you." She smiled up at him.

"Oh? The man is hard to read."

"Maybe." She followed him on the slow circuit of the floor, drifting with him and teasing herself with a desire that had hours to go before they could fulfill it. "But unlike everyone else I danced with tonight, all he wanted to discuss was his admiration for your work."

"Really? That was kind of him. All anyone else wants to talk about is how beautiful you are." The compliment wrapped her up in an embrace that almost matched the warmth surrounding her from his arms.

"I find that hard to believe. These men look so serious." She teased, but it wasn't a joke, exactly. Most of the men in attendance at the party wore smart suits, buttoned down and engaged in earnest discussions. The subjects included everything from financial recovery to advertising methods to penetrate a dense market and of course, the challenges that arose in the wake of the natural disaster that nearly cost them their corporate data.

Despite Daniel's assertion, his name came up in every conversation—his name and the reliability of Spherecast to develop the right software for the right problem. He was the star tonight and she couldn't be prouder.

"Want to know a secret?" His lips brushed her ear.

"Is that a trick question?" One song dovetailed into the next and despite his assurance to his host, he seemed to have no intention of leaving her yet.

"Martin told me Takahashi approached him with an exclusive offer to use only Spherecast software. It'll take about a year to transition all their systems, rewrite some code and get it working, but he *is* interested."

"Daniel, that's amazing." She cupped his face in her hands, her heart swelled for him. She hadn't missed the hours he'd poured into this project. Despite all the programmers and developers working for him, he'd dedicated dozens of long nights to perfecting the program.

"It's pretty awesome." He grinned again, twirling her a little faster than the music called for. "I'll have to go to Tokyo in a couple of months. Do you like sushi?"

Martin appeared at their elbows and she swallowed her answer. "Sorry to interrupt you lovebirds, but Takahashi would like to sit down with you now, Daniel."

The nervous flutters in her stomach beat a rhythm and she squeezed his arms. "You can do this." She didn't know why she felt the urge to encourage him, but his quick inhalation and the taut flex of his throat suggested he was a lot more nervous than he let on. He stilled, gazing into her eyes, and his expression relaxed, a smile warming his lips before he brushed her mouth with a whisper of a kiss.

"Thank you."

"I'll be here when you get back." A promise.

"You better be." He squeezed her hand and then he was gone, striding across the room, every inch the confident sun god who blew into her life and turned it upside down. Pride shimmered through her as she watched him greet the executives and they trickled out to a private conference room. He took Martin with him—she trusted the lawyer to look after him. Jittery with nerves, she accepted a glass of wine from the waitress and murmured a thank-you. Sipping the alcohol, she drifted across the room to the great paned windows that looked out over the glittering jewel of Los Angeles's nightscape.

It was easy to forget that beneath the smog and glamour pulsed a very real city. Standing inside the tower, she could see all the way to the ocean. It was a rare, clear view, the Santa Ana winds having pushed all the tendrils of haze away, leaving the night gleaming with spotlights, strobes and towers that reached up like fingers to stroke the stars.

"Your Highness? Please pardon the intrusion."

No matter how much she practiced with Victor, it was always a jolt when someone else said it. She glanced up at the reflection in the glass behind her. She didn't recognize the gentleman, so she turned, a polite smile on her face. "Please, call me Alyx or Miss Dagmar. It's a little less of a mouthful than Your Highness." And so much easier to respond to, but she avoided adding the caveat.

"Miss Dagmar. My name is Richard Prentiss." He withdrew a card and handed it to her. She glanced down at the heavily embossed cardstock. The symbol in the corner was an elegant crest— one she recognized.

It represented her family.

She studied him. He didn't resemble any of the photos she'd memorized nor did his features suggest a personal relationship with her. "Mr. Prentiss, it's a pleasure to make your acquaintance." Extending her hand, she wasn't surprised when he bowed over it and brushed a kiss lightly to the air over one knuckle. It was a kind, respectful greeting.

"And a rare pleasure to make yours. I understand that you are attending this function to support your fiancé, Mr. Voldakov."

She didn't have to manufacture the soft smile curving her lips. "Yes, he's done some wonderful work for the Takahashi Corporation and they are showing him a rare honor with this party. I would introduce you, but..." She motioned to the conference room Daniel vanished into.

"I would enjoy such an introduction but I am actually here for two reasons and I hope you'll forgive the minor subterfuge."

Sipping the wine, she resisted the urge to rub her suddenly damp palms against her dress. What subterfuge? The vellum card weighed heavily in her hand. Instead, she focused on breathing, calm, and canting her head to suggest a hint of patient curiosity. Hours of drills with Victor paid off in that moment. "And what subterfuge would that be, Mr. Prentiss?"

The man had the good grace to flush, a hint of red staining his ears. "To inquire whether you would accept an invitation from your cousin, His Highness, the Grand Duke Armand."

My cousin.

A second jolt in as many minutes and her confidence wavered. The grand duke divided his time between his native Norway and France most of the year. The newspapers referred to him as a playboy, often featuring photographs of the prince with a host of women at various functions throughout Europe.

"Because an invitation cannot be extended if I will not accept." It was a statement, not a question. Protocol demanded that no one could turn down the royal family, whether they were a displaced one or not. It was how the royals played. Kind of weird, but then who wanted to be rejected?

"Precisely, Your Highness, and I apologize for putting you on the spot. His Highness recognizes that you may be reluctant to see him and asked that I extend to you his deepest desire to make your acquaintance. If you could see it in your heart to accept his invitation, he would like a chance to speak with you in person." There was a subtext to his words, a suggestion that the grand duke wanted to do more than just talk to *her*. The jittery butterflies in her stomach flapped harder. This was exactly the type of invitation Daniel wanted, the reason he'd approached her. Access to the grand duke and his European connections could help him launch Spherecast's influence in the EU.

So why did she hesitate?

"I'm not entirely sure what my schedule is." That seemed the safest answer and her heart beat against her ribs so hard, she was certain he could hear it. "But if you would let me pass this card to my assistant, I can have him get in touch with you." She tucked the card into her clutch, careful to make sure it slid inside before she snapped the little purse closed.

"Absolutely." Prentiss's expression relaxed and he smiled. "Which brings us to the second reason for my approach."

The reminder that he had two reasons ramped her already emotionally unsettled state closer to full-blown panic. She took another sip of the wine and prayed the alcohol would relax the jangling of her nerves. Amazingly, her voice didn't betray a quaver. "I am filled with curiosity."

Prentiss actually grinned at that, some of the stiffness leaving his shoulders. Dark haired and dark eyed, he cut a striking image in his equally dark suit, but she cataloged his looks more from a clinical standpoint.

His darkness couldn't compete with the sunshine in Daniel.

"To give you a gift. Your birthday is approaching and whether you accept the invitation or not, the grand duke wanted you to have this."

He held out a small box, wrapped in a simple gold foil. She had to set her wineglass down and slipped her clutch purse's strap over her shoulder to take the box. Eagerness flared inside, pushing away the anxiety. "I'm surprised he would send such a gift, considering we have never met." Maybe it wasn't politically correct to say such a thing, but the sentiment remained genuine.

"He has many years to make up for and while this simple gift cannot possibly repair such a history of oversight, he hopes that you will wear it with the pride you should. His words, exactly, Highness." Prentiss gave her another kind look and party or not, she slid one manicured nail through the tape and revealed a velvet jewelry box. She wasn't really sure of the protocol of such a thing but she wanted to know. She glanced at him before lifting the lid. Inside nestled a lovely cameo on a silver strand. But instead of a profile, it was her family crest set against a background of royal blue.

The breath caught in her throat and tears swam across her vision. "How can he accept me? Just like that?" She forgot about the rules, the manners and the control she'd worked to perfect.

"You are the image of your great-grand-mother, Your Highness. If you'll look beneath the necklace, he included a small photo of her. He has no doubts that you are indeed the grand duchess and he is most eager to welcome you to the family."

The tears prickling her eyes threatened to spill. She chewed at her bottom lip and blinked at him. Prentiss shifted with just the barest hint of discomfort. Daniel appeared in her periphery, an arm snaking around her waist.

"Are you all right?" He murmured the words to her, but set a hard look on the attorney.

She gave a watery little laugh and nodded, holding the necklace over to show him. "Daniel, this is Richard Prentiss, he's—I'm not sure if you work for him or are just associated with the grand duke?" She glanced back to Prentiss.

"I'm a personal friend. Armand and I went to university together." He extended a hand to Daniel, who accepted it only briefly, but continued to stare at him until Prentiss cleared his throat and retreated a step. "If you will excuse me, Your Highness, Mr. Voldakov. I will await your assistant's call."

"Yes." She tried to clear her throat, embarrassed at the tears leaking from the corners of her eyes. "Thank you and please—please—pass my thanks on to the grand duke as well." She made a second attempt to get around the lump in her throat, but too much clogged it. The tenderness from Daniel cuddling her side, the weight of the family necklace in her hands and the encouragement of a man she'd never met who accepted her as a member of his family.

Her head spun from all of it.

Prentiss excused himself and Daniel circled around to block her from the rest of the room. He held out a handkerchief and she dabbed at her eyes again, trying to quell the unfamiliar tears.

"Are you sure you're okay?" He frowned.

"I'm fine. Really—I think I'm more than fine. I wasn't—I wasn't expecting anyone to approach me tonight, you know, not from him. He's my cousin—third cousin once removed or something like that. I've lost track of how all that works. But he wants to meet me and more than that—" she held up the necklace, tears threatening again, "—whether I want to see him or not, he sent this as a token to acknowledge me as a member of the family and for my birthday."

"Your birthday..." Daniel exhaled and she saw his pained look. He'd not realized. "When is it?"

"Oh, that's not important. I don't know why

this is getting to me so much." She really didn't. Why should a stranger's approval touch her so deeply?

Her thumb traced the crest. Before three months ago, before Daniel, she'd never heard of the Andraste royal line, much less imagined herself a part of it. She was a waitress working her ass off between auditions, an actress desperate to make her mark and break out of the fifty-dollar-a-day extra jobs.

Now she was the Grand Duchess Alyxandretta and none of Victor's lessons could prepare her for the weight of that responsibility.

"Well, I beg to differ. It is important." Daniel closed his hand over hers on the necklace. "In the meantime, contracts have been proposed and it's up to Martin to hammer it all out. Want to run away with me for a while?"

She sniffled and grinned. "Running away to Beverly Hills isn't exactly running away."

"No—but I was thinking a little further. Ever been to Big Bear?"

Having repaired most of the tear damage, she shook her head slowly. "No."

"Me either. Wanna go?" His eagerness must have been contagious, because she no sooner nodded than he threaded her arm through his and they cruised through the room. Quick pleasantries, glad handing a few executives and they were at the door, claiming her wrap.

As she stepped into the elevator, she caught sight of Prentiss's gentle smile and he lifted his wineglass in quiet salute. She inclined her head and let out a squeaky breath as the doors whooshed closed.

As if by mutual consent, Daniel caught her face in his hands and his lips slanted over hers, a hot salty kiss that smashed through the wobbly barriers, already raw from the grand duke's invitation and Daniel's success. She clung to him, arms twining around his shoulders. A clatter of noise pushed between them as the doors opened and a couple of photographers snapped their photos. The flashes dazzled her eyes. Daniel lifted his head with a mild oath and tucked her into his side.

Building security appeared and escorted the photographers away, but more waited in front of the building. The flashes cut through the dark evening and she hid her face against Daniel's shoulder as he guided them through the throng and to the open door of the limo. The driver closed them in and hurried around to pull away.

"Holy crap." She glanced back at the crowd on the sidewalk.

"Yeah, I know. But let's forget them." Daniel grinned and tugged her to him. She met his lips with a sigh and dropped the necklace box onto the seat. He palmed the privacy control and the window to the driver slid shut. When his hands shaped over her breasts, she let out a little moan.

"In the car?" Breathless laughter rose up. She was still seeing stars from the flashes.

"Oh, yeah. In the car. On the car." A zipper on the side of her dress gave way and he hiked her skirt up. Dampness flooded between her legs and she could feel the weight of his erection pressing up to her as he tugged her onto his lap. "Right here. Right now."

"But the driver—" This was insane. They'd just been in the middle of a formal party and the grand duke sent someone to approach her. Everything about that event had been foreign to her just weeks earlier.

He cut her off with another tongue-thrusting kiss. She forgot about the necklace, the photographers and the driver. It took a little juggling to get his pants open and she teased his cock as she helped him into a condom. There was something so lovely about the silken heat of his skin as she rolled the condom into place.

Once it was fitted to him, he closed his hand over hers and she rose a little higher so they could line his cock up. There was a little jolt and she bumped her head against the roof before she could sink down. Still laughing, she made a face at Daniel and then he was inside of her, stretching her perfectly.

"The driver," she gasped out in between kisses. "Is he going to know?"

"Who cares?" He palmed her breast as he thrust upward. Pleasure licked lazy flames through her as she braced her hands against his shoulders. "He's paid by the hour. He can drive us around all night."

That pulled another laugh from her. "Pretty sure Victor would frown at the etiquette." His next thrust upward pushed the air from her lungs.

"Do you want me to stop?" The question whispered against her lips sent a cascade of feeling through her.

"Absolutely not," she said, her tone probably sharper than it needed to be. Then again, she also fisted his hair as she rolled her hips, taking her cue for the rhythm from him.

"Thank God," he muttered.

"Daniel..." But his kiss swallowed the rest of her words.

I love you.

CHAPTER 18
ALYX

S adly, they had to put off Big Bear for a couple of days. It turned out Daniel actually did have meetings he couldn't just cancel. His grousing about being the boss made her laugh.

"It'll be fine," she told him. "It gives me time to pick out stuff to pack."

"You don't need to pack anything," he said, tangling his fingers with hers. "I don't plan on us needing to be dressed from the moment we get there until the moment we leave."

Well, that sent a flutter through her. "I like an ambitious man."

His grin was a flash of sunlight piercing his petulant mood and washing it away. When he leaned over to brush a kiss to her lips, she sighed into it. They'd been lovers for barely a week, but it felt so damn natural.

Natural and wanted.

More, she treasured the way he studied her face like he was trying to memorize it before he left. With a soft stroke of his thumb along her cheekbone, he sighed. "Theresa will be doing the shopping today. If you need anything…"

"I can go out and get it myself," she reminded him. "In fact, I might go out today and see a friend." The lessons with Victor had slowed the last three weeks. So that wasn't something she had to worry about. "Do you think you'll be late?"

"I better not be," he said with a grumble. "But if I am, I'll call or message."

"That works," she covered his hand on her cheek with his "I'll message you if I'm delayed too. I figure I can call Rhonda and bribe her into lunch with me."

She didn't miss the way relief rippled through his expression. He hadn't asked who she was going to see, but he'd wanted too. The tension that had ticked in his jaw also went away.

"Hmm, if you need reservations somewhere, call Lucy. She'll get you in anywhere you want to go." Still, he stood there, as though truly hesitant to leave.

"You're going to spoil me," she teased.

"You have discovered my nefarious plan."

Now, she snorted. "Not particularly nefarious, but I'll let it go this time. Yes, if I need reservations, I'll call Lucy." She liked Lucy. The older woman was actually entertaining when she scolded Daniel. The fact he clearly adored the secretary didn't hurt.

"Well that's a relief." Then he kissed her hand. "Do something for me?"

Her stomach clenched a little tighter and an icy sensation skated over her skin. "If I can..."

"Take one of my cars instead of yours?" The fact she still had her car was a small bone of contention. He'd had his mechanic look at it and fix it up. He'd also had it cleaned, but he didn't like the lack of amenities. "The Mercedes or the Volvo... or better, I can arrange a car for you."

She held up a finger. "I don't want a driver, but I will take one of your cars." It was as far as she was willing to compromise. "I will also be careful. I don't plan on alerting anyone to where I am going that isn't you, Rhonda, or Lucy."

Hell, she and Rhonda might just have lunch at Rhonda's.

Blowing out a breath, he ducked his head to give her another kiss. "Okay, I'll let you know if I'm late." It seemed a concession, he didn't like her going out on her own. But it was well past time. She'd spent the last few months either here or with Victor or Daniel.

There'd been no Alyx time and Alyx needed the time.

"I'll see you later," she called and he gave her one more smile before his phone rang and he answered it on his way out.

"Hey Martin, just leaving now..."

❦

"So, this guy is a lawyer who works for the royal guy who is your cousin?" Rhonda asked as she stretched her legs out and propped her feet on the railing of her balcony. It was a gorgeous day out and the breeze just made it even better.

"Pretty much, said his name was Richard Prentiss. I googled him. So he's the real deal. Well, at least real in the sense that he has a law firm and he is a member of the bar." I tipped the icy bottle of soda back for a long drink. We'd walked down to a food truck we both enjoyed and grabbed Mexican food, sodas, and treats before coming back to eat lunch here. "I also found photos of him with Armand Andraste."

Which had also quieted some nerves and ignited others. A part of her really hadn't believed Daniel. Even all these weeks later, she still struggled to believe it was even possible. To have a man she'd never met acknowledge her that way was—she couldn't really find the words to express it.

"No shit?" Rhonda said, tugging her sunglasses off. "Like for real, for real?"

"Yeah, for real. It's crazy, right?"

Now she just gaped at me. "Moving in with some guy you just met and pretending to be his fiancee was fucking crazy, Alyx. This? This is some fairy tale shit."

She wasn't wrong and Alyx's stomach did a crazy twist as ice coated the back of her neck. Instead of answering, she took another swallow of the pineapple Jarritos she'd gotten for herself.

"Hey..." Rhonda reached over to put her hand on Alyx's arm. "You okay?"

"Yes?" she said, quite trusting her own voice at the moment. "No? I don't know. Yes, you said I was nuts to take the gig, but Daniel's been great. Even Victor, who is kind of a dick, is pretty good too."

"But?" The older woman prompted, her gaze fixed on Alyx.

"But... you're right, this is some fairy tale stuff and it's hard to believe. Good shit like this doesn't happen to me." I raised the drink and took another long swallow. The sweet and the tart helped to quench the sudden dryness in her throat. "I haven't reached out yet."

"What does your guy think?" Rhonda never said his name. It was like she kept him at arms length. Complaining about it didn't change her mind and it kind of let her look at everything from the distance. Maybe Alyx needed her to do that.

"Daniel?" She had to ask though because they'd been discussing Richard and Armand.

The bland look Rhonda shot Alyx made her laugh. Maybe Alyx shouldn't think it was so funny, but it was damn entertaining on some levels.

"He hasn't said anything, really." After downing another swallow, she turned her gaze over the view of the parking lot and swimming pool. "We talked about it a little that night of the party, then he asked me if I wanted to go up to Big Bear."

She rolled the bottle in circles between her palms.

"It's like pulling teeth," Rhonda complained. "What did he say?"

"Just he was, you know glad for me, and then did I want to go to Big Bear. It was a huge night for him, he's got this deal going on with this Japanese company and there was a lovely party. Then Mr. Prentiss showing up and giving me that cameo..."

"Cameo? Wait, I think you left that part out."

Had she? "Sorry." She took a moment to bring her up to speed about the cameo and the family crest. "It's really beautiful and it's a really amazing acknowledgment. It kind of overwhelmed me. I almost burst into tears right there."

"I bet," Rhonda said with a sigh. "So you leave and your guy just asks about Big Bear? He doesn't say call the attorney? Make an appointment with the duke or prince or whatever he is?"

No, he hadn't. "To be fair, he's been really busy since then. The deal with the Japanese company. The meetings and he had a lot of them or we'd have already gone to Big Bear." A little laugh escaped her. "He's kind of grumpy about that, but we're going to go this weekend."

"Wasn't the whole point of this to get an introduction to this prince—Armand person?" She made a play out of his name and I gave a little shrug. It had been...

"That's still a goal," she said slowly. "But he's not pushing me to reach out and maybe that's better you know."

"Uh huh." Skepticism riffled through the word. "He stalks you, sets you up with the weird audition, then offers you a ridiculous amount of

211

money to play Holly Golightly so he can make nice with aristocracy and get his foot in the door."

She couldn't really argue with Rhonda's assessment. "That is the way it started, but we've become real friends—"

"Oh, honey," Rhonda said, a wealth of disappointment in those two words. Disappointment and sympathy. "Sweetheart, don't tell me you fell for him?"

"I said we're friends." Even if she'd almost said I love you, she hadn't. "He's been really good to me. Not everything worked out, but he did try to help me get things from my parents."

That whole episode still made her want to cry. Before Daniel, she'd stopped believing in good things and "fairy tale shit" as Rhonda called it. Maybe she was still skeptical now, but he'd *tried*.

It had to mean something.

Being lovers was...

Scrubbing a hand over her face, Rhonda shook her head. "Sweetheart, promise me if you're sleeping with that man that you're taking precautions. Yes, he might seem great right now, but you still have something he wants. Once he gets it? What then?"

Opening her mouth, she considered her response then closed it again. Finally, she just said, "We haven't really talked about that. Not since we signed the contract. The contract is for a year."

They still had another nine months...

"Yes, I'm being careful." Irritation scraped through her now. "Maybe taking our time is a good thing. He's not rushing to get to the prince. That could mean he doesn't want this to end too."

Rhonda said nothing but her silence seemed particularly heavy.

"I promise," Alyx said, reassuring both of them. "I know what I'm doing and I'm being careful."

"Has it occurred to you that no matter what you do, the life you used to have is done now?" The quiet words said aloud the things Alyx had been trying to not think about. "One month or one year with this guy and maybe you do end the contract, you with your spiffy new family and his with all his money and access—you both get what you want."

The way she searched Alyx's face made that last part seem far more of a question than a statement.

"I've seen you on the gossip sites. I've seen the little clips here and there... You won't just be Alyx Dagmar, waitress and aspiring actress. That part is over."

Alyx blew out a breath.

"I hope you're ready for that, whether the guy is a part of it or not."

As much as she wanted to assure her, Alyx really didn't know the answer. That sinking feeling didn't go away, even when they changed the subject. It circled her like dark water in a whirlpool, sucking down her mood. It lingered long after Alyx left to go back to Daniel's place.

He pulled in right behind her. It was impossible to miss the wide grin he shot her. In fact, no sooner has she parked than he was at the driver's side door and tugging her out of the vehicle.

"Hey," she said.

"Hey." His smile didn't diminish as he pulled her close. His kiss absolutely robbed her of breath and smothered all the dark, restless thoughts. Wrapping her arms around him, she banished all those questions to a dark corner and locked them away.

They could deal with it later.

CHAPTER 19
DANIEL

He woke to the feeling of her hands on his chest.

Three days...

Three days of hiding away at a cabin in Big Bear and all he had to do was look at her to feel his pulse quicken. He never wanted to leave. They'd stayed up late, feeding each other ice cream and watching another marathon of *Red Dwarf* episodes. Episodes they repeatedly had to start over. Particularly after the whipped cream dripped onto her breast... He grinned at that memory. He preferred his whipped cream with nipple on top.

Telling her as much had earned him a shocked look and a delicious peal of laughter that squeezed his orgasm out of him.

Daniel sighed, shifting against the pillows and adjusting her so she seemed more comfortable. Her rich red hair trailed across his chest and her face relaxed completely into slumber with her lips still swollen from kissing him all night long.

This was the purest definition of perfect.

No, he amended mentally, his gaze tracking up to the beat-up bear sitting on the nightstand on her side of the bed. The drive there had been hurried, a rush to escape from the business of home and to lock themselves away in a sweet escape.

He hadn't questioned his own impatience or taken a look at motivations. Walking out of that meeting with Takahashi to see her stricken expression as a stranger leaned into her set off every alarm bell in his head. He'd marched over there, fighting the first real urge to violence he'd ever experienced. The need to shield her had expanded to be so all-consuming, he'd just wanted to get her out of there, then away from the house. Away from where anyone might find her.

The fact he'd been prevented from leaving for several more days had been infuriating. Each day he'd had to say goodbye to her while he went to the office had eaten away at him. Prentiss had called his office once. He had Lucy put him off. The deal with Takahashi took all of his attention. As soon as it was all finalized, they could steal away.

Prentiss and the duke could wait.

Alyx shifted and her leg nestled deeper between his. He grinned as her mouth opened and closed, a hint of a kiss brushing his pec. It was ridiculous just how deep he'd fallen for this woman. The fact that the grand duke made his approach should have him crowing about financial good fortune, but all he could think about were the tears in her eyes, the absolute blown-away expression on her face and the traces of fear in her voice.

She couldn't imagine why someone would want her or reach out to her.

He couldn't imagine not having her right where she was—in his arms.

That was why he'd wanted her away. Maybe they could extend their absence. Another week here, or a trip to Napa. Their last trip there had been amazing.

The photographers closing in, the messages from Lucy about press calls and Martin's satisfaction about how well his insane plan worked echoed in the back of his mind. Daniel had wanted to crown her a princess, but it never occurred to him that changing her life meant he'd really changed it. Business deal or not, when all was said and done, she would still be a princess. The press would be there, demands for her attention would only continue to increase if the world fell half as much in love with her as he was.

The sobering thought sent adrenaline surging through him. The urge to take her somewhere it could be just the two of them flooded through him so strongly that he'd rushed her into the car as soon as the very last meeting had been handled. She'd only pushed back long enough to grab her bear from her car. She didn't care about clothes or supplies, but she wanted her bear. Even as the thought occurred to him, his gaze landed on the nightstand.

The ratty one-eyed, overstitched bear sat like a monarch on his nightstand throne.

That bear made this perfect.

She'd carried him in from the car, setting the bear in the room they shared now for real. Their room. Their bed. Their time together.

The ridiculous soppy sentiment prickled through him and he twisted, turning her over to nuzzle her cheek. Like a kid at Christmas, he didn't want to wait for her to wake up.

Her arms wrapped around him and she murmured against his lips, "Good morning."

"Morning." He deepened the kiss, inviting her tongue to dance with his. Her foot slid along the back of his leg and his stiff cock glided against the wet heat of her sex.

For the barest moment, the idea of skipping a condom and just burrowing into her body tried to take root. If he could fill her with a baby, she wouldn't go anywhere, but he shook away the thought. She'd lost enough choices in her life and as much as he longed to tie her to him, it had to be her choice.

"Did you get any sleep?" Her drowsy voice stroked over his senses like hot dark chocolate poured over a cold treat, sensuous and inviting. He nibbled along her lower lip, drawing it between his teeth and answering her with another soul-baring kiss.

"Some," he murmured, tracing a path to her ear and then down the slender column of her throat. He nipped at the steady pulse beating beneath her skin. Her pebbled nipples stabbed at his chest and reminded him that he had so much more to play with. He continued his descent, enjoying her low sigh as he circled one nipple with his tongue. Blowing cool air, he grinned at the red tip pearling tight just for him. "But this is so much more interesting than sleep."

He latched on to the nipple and thrummed it with his tongue. Moments later, as she arched up to him, he rolled a condom on and sank into the hot clamp of her pussy. She let out a low cry, legs scissoring around his waist. The urgency to take her quieted only to be replaced by the singular purpose of burying himself so deeply in her she would forget they'd ever been two people.

She gazed up at him. Her hands stroked up and down his sides in time to his thrusts and a smile played on her lips. "I don't want this to ever end."

"It never has to." He promised and sealed the oath with another kiss before letting himself get lost in the feel of her. The orgasm that shot through him left them clinging together. Slippery with sweat, he rolled onto his back and draped her across him, enjoying the way her hair curtained around him.

This is perfect.

"I'm hungry," she announced with a half yawn and more than impish grin. As if to illustrate her point, her stomach growled.

He chuckled. "Ride me to exhaustion and then demand to be fed. I see how you are."

She propped her chin in her hand and lifted her eyebrows. "I beg to differ. You kept me up all night and then woke me up to ride me to exhaustion. You need to feed me or I may perish from fine sex." The wicked twinkle in her eyes sent a wave of humor through him.

"Well, I would not want you to perish from fine sex."

"Good. Because I believe I've finally acquired the taste for it." She studied him, her lashes dropping to cover her eyes. "A very specific taste—which means you'll have to work to keep me pleased."

"I see. And what does my princess want for food this morning?" He pinched her bottom, grunting as she flexed around him and jerked.

God, it hurt so good.

Her outraged laughter, however, was music to his ears. "I want pancakes. Big fat, fluffy pancakes."

"Hmm..." He massaged the buttock he'd pinched, rubbing his palm against her skin. He really liked her ass. He loved squeezing it as she took him inside her. "That means getting up and getting dressed."

"We have to get out of this bed sometime."

He considered it. And slid out of her and rolled her over so he could look at her back, teasing a line of kisses down her shoulder. "No, we don't." He gave her rump a little smack when she started to rise. "Stay put."

After disposing of the condom, he found his cell phone and called down to the lodge. His cabin was nestled into a private area of the resort, hidden away and secure. He ordered up pancakes, bacon, orange juice and coffee and told them to deliver it in forty-five minutes. She stayed on her tummy, but shot him a questioning look. "I'm hungry now."

Grinning at the plaintive whine, he slid back onto the bed behind her and nudged her legs apart. "So am I, and I seem to remember promising to go down on you." Her startled squeal, then low sigh, was all the reward he needed as he flicked his tongue out for a taste. She was just as sweet and spicy as he remembered.

~

IT WAS lunchtime before he heated up the pancakes and served her in the bed. She looked like a queen, draped out and exhausted. He wasn't sure where all his need to take her came from, the urge to fill her up, to keep touching her, to never be apart. Maybe the fact that the press and world noticing his princess meant they would try to take her away from him.

After all, he'd only secured her time for the year.

Grimacing at that thought, he stared down at his pancakes moodily.

"Hey." She nudged him with a foot along his leg. Whisker burns reddened the sides of her breasts and her cheeks. He really needed to shave before he touched her again. "What's wrong?"

"Nothing," he lied with a quick shake of his head. "Just—just business stuff." He wanted to tear up the contract. Martin would kill him, but that was exactly what he needed to do. Tear it up and give her the shredded copy.

Then get down on one knee and ask her to stay for real. Not for money. Not for business.

But for him.

The thought cheered him somewhat and he dredged up a smile. "I'm going to shower and shave—" Her fingers stroking his cheek stilled the next words and he looked at her questioningly.

"I kind of like my sun gods scruffy." The sultry words went straight to his cock and it gave a valiant attempt to firm up.

"Sun god, huh?"

"Oh yeah." Her fingers rasped against the stubble. "Blond hair, blue eyes, bronze skin and a killer smile. Definitely a sun god."

"Thank you. But the scruffy keeps marking your skin and I don't want to hurt you." *In any way.*

She leaned back against the pillows and nibbled her last slice of bacon. She was so unabashed in her nudity, one knee up, her breasts full and lush and utterly kissable. God, if he sat here much longer he'd forget about the shower and remind them both why he needed to shave.

Stacking the plates together, he set them on the table. "I'll be right back."

"I hate to see you go, but I love watching you walk away." He could feel her gaze on him all the way across the room and he resisted the urge to puff out his chest. But when he paused in the bathroom door to look back at her, he couldn't help but grin at her wolf whistle.

"You're terrible," he accused her, still smiling.

"You love it," she teased, wrinkling her nose.

"Oh yeah." He swept his gaze over her. "I do."

Her little inhale sent another grin to his lips as he stepped into the bathroom. He met his gaze in the mirror and nodded. Everything would change when they went home. Shred the contract, talk her into staying and turn this charade into the real thing. Princess or not, deal or not—he wanted Alyx.

Fear punched him in the gut.

But does she want me?

~

ALYX

The bathroom door closed behind him and Alyx rocked up to hug her knees. Her heart beat triple time. She'd teased him about loving her, but the look in his eyes, the way he agreed and said *I do...* Her insides knotted up.

She'd fallen for him, hook, line and glass slipper. But the Daniel she fell for wasn't the one paying the bills or writing a check—it was the crazy man knocking on her car window. The sensitive guy who seemed truly troubled by the fact that she slept in her car. The thoughtful one who took her to Sacramento to search for her past. The crazy guy who made love to her in the backseat of a limo. The playful one who pinched her bottom and tickled her even as he made love to her.

It was the Daniel who stayed up all night to fix a software problem because it helped someone or shared ice cream and silly stories with her in his kitchen. It was the protective Daniel who stood up to Victor. And—God help her—the passionate one who kissed her until the rest of the world faded away.

But does he mean it? Or has he just fallen for the image we've been creating?

Self-doubt was a cold bed companion and it crawled across their passion-scented sheets to wrap its icy fingers around her spine. As much as she'd tried to not obsess over it, Rhonda's words and doubt haunted her. She looked at the bathroom and listened to the sound of the water. Sliding forward, she started off the bed to join him—to ask him. She'd never been a coward and she wasn't going to start acting like one now, but a buzzing interrupted her. His cell phone sat next to the bed and Martin's name flashed on the caller ID.

Ignore it, she told herself, but hesitated. It could be important. Daniel had kept his phone off for most of their sojourn at Big Bear. They'd actually been followed part of the way by photographers—a first and totally unwelcome experience—but once on the resort property, they were safe behind security gates.

On the fourth buzzing vibration, she scooped up the phone. "Hello, Martin. He's in the shower. Is it important?"

"Well, Princess, it's definitely fantastic news, but I can tell you and you can tell him. How's that sound?" Martin didn't sound like the tough, cynical lawyer she'd first spoken to. His guarded tone was gone, replaced by one that was almost giddy.

She wanted to say no, call him later. But she'd answered the phone.

In for a penny... So she exhaled and said, "Sure. What's going on?"

"The Grand Duke Armand and his retinue will be in Los Angeles tonight and have requested the honor of your presence—both of you—at a private gala for the family and a few close business associates."

Her stomach plummeted at the news, but Martin continued on, oblivious to the ice creeping around her heart.

"But that's not all. Spherecast has been scouted by an EU consortium—the same one your cousin heads. They've invited us to a demonstration at the Brussels conference next month." She could practically hear the fist pump in his words. "This is a real coup, Alyx. A real coup. I know you weren't that thrilled on this when Daniel proposed his insane idea—and neither was I." His conversational tone took on an almost confidential note, as if they'd truly been aligned on this matter from the beginning. "But you did it. The two of you have completely sold the world on your romance and escaping to Big Bear—genius. I thought he was crazy to really play up the romance, but it's worked. Online and off, it's all the social media hawks have been able to talk about. Where you've gone, the beauty of your romance—and now the grand duke..." He sighed. "Thank you, from the bottom line to the headlines, thank you for doing this for him. I told him to buy a royal bloodline and he did it. Now, get your butts back to L.A. and that party tonight. Invitation says cocktails will be served at seven."

She wasn't aware of the tears until they dripped onto her bare thighs. "Okay, we'll be there." But Martin had already hung up. She looked at the phone for a long time. God, she was such a fool.

This was exactly what Daniel had wanted. Right. It was the deal she agreed to, and she promised to do her job.

Daniel had pursued her to become a princess and she'd become one. The media noticed, his friends noticed and her long-distance-don't-really-know-them family noticed.

From their first kiss to the first time they'd made love—it had been all about being a princess, a princess in love. They'd put on a grand show.

Too grand.

I thought he was crazy to really play up the romance, but it's worked.

She swiped at her tears angrily. Somehow she'd fallen for the dream, the ideal they were constructing. She'd started to believe in the charade. The fairy tale shit as Rhonda put it.

She knew better. Good things like this didn't happen. It was more like what happened to her things, forgotten, lost, and discarded. Like her.

"I knew not to do this. It's why I said no sex to begin with." The anger pouring out was all directed to herself. Daniel falling for her as a princess wasn't his fault. She let him play the game—reveled in the seduction. "Idiot."

Pushing off the bed, she refused to look at the rumpled sheets. She was dressed in ten minutes and tying on her tennis shoes. The shower continued to run, so she picked up the phone and called the front desk to order a car. The drive to Los Angeles would take a couple of hours, but if he was to seal the deal, he needed the Princess Alyxandretta on his arm, not the thoroughly disheveled lover with nothing but shorts, T-shirts and jeans at her disposal. The desk promised to send a car for him. She'd keep her word and make sure his dream happened for him.

His keys sat on the desk. She found a pen and took the coward's way out—she wrote Daniel a note.

The grand duke is in Los Angeles. Martin called. Your deal is on. We have to be there. Taking the car. I need to get ready and will meet you at the "ball." Called for a car to drive you back—lots to do so I won't disappoint you.

Adding the location and the time of the event she sniffled and signed it with just an *A*. She set the note on the pillow and circled the bed to grab her bear.

There was nothing else for her in the cabin— just a dream that she'd let herself believe in for five minutes.

If only she could learn her lesson. At the door,

she hesitated again. It wouldn't take her long to tell him the message in person, but the water continued to run and his keys were heavy in her hand.

She needed to get the hell out while she still remembered who she was.

No, he'd hired her to be a princess and to help him enter the European market. It was time to live up to her end of the bargain without any strings or emotional attachments. She buried her pain under a veil of practicality. She'd managed for years without anything—or anyone—of her own.

She could do it again.

But once she was in the car and headed toward Los Angeles, all she could think about was Daniel. Daniel at his desk. Daniel in their—his bed. Holding her. Smiling at her. Teasing her.

Alone, she could cry.

Even princesses can be fools.

CHAPTER 20
ALYX

"Your Highness." Victor frowned as he eyed her red-splotched face. "You cannot continue to tell me nothing is wrong."

"It's really not important, Victor, and I would prefer it if you could just call me Alyx from now on. You did your job, I'm Her Highness in the papers, and Princess or Grand Duchess or whatever it is they want to call me." She smoothed down the black dress. She'd considered the red or the blue, but elected for the simple spaghetti-strapped black velvet sheath that fell to her ankles. The split on the right leg was perfectly respectable, stopping just above the knee. In the black Manolo Blahniks, she would present a classic appearance.

She'd called Victor to meet her at the dress shop after she took the time to get her hair done. All that was left were her cosmetics and she still had an hour before she was due at the grand duke's hotel.

Victor snapped his fingers and the two

women who'd been assisting him stepped out of the room. Closing the door, he leaned back against it and folded his arms. "No, it is important. You've been crying on and off for hours. Your eyes are puffy, your nose is red and your voice is thick with the clog of tears. I cannot help you if you don't tell me what's wrong."

As if to illustrate his point, she grabbed some tissue and turned away to blow her nose. "There's nothing you can do, except maybe help me fix this bride-of-Frankenstein face."

"Princess." It must have been her imagination, but the cool brisk tones of her acting coach softened with gentle sympathy. The tears leaked out all over again.

"Don't do that." She sniffled.

"Do what?" He looked genuinely baffled.

"Be nice. Don't be nice." She pressed the tissue to her nose and turned around to face him. "Tell me to put my chin up and my shoulders back. Remind me that posture is important and that my tone of voice should always indicate interest no matter how dreadful the conversation. When I am outside this room, I am always on display and no one is to be trusted, not even my closest advisors, because royal stories sell whether I'm a real royal or not."

A brief smile touched his lips. "Why should I have to remind you, Princess? The student has become the master. It has shown in every image taken of you. You walk with grace, you speak with poise and now, amidst all these dreadful tears, you stand as if you should be noticed."

A watery laugh bubbled up. "That's not helping either." She dabbed at her eyes and fanned her face. She was so hot. Her cheeks blazed with it and her eyes burned. She was a dreadful crier and her red nose felt twice its normal size.

"Talk to me about it. Let out what is eating your soul apart inside. Perhaps it is not as bad as you think it is." The cool, practical teacher was back, but the empathy in his eyes begged her to tell him everything.

"I shouldn't gossip with the staff." She sniffled and then chuckled.

"True. For the next—" he glanced at his watch, "—twenty minutes, I quit. I am no longer in your employ. I am merely a man who once taught you and would very much like to be your friend."

"Really?" Did he mean it or was this just another acting lesson?

"Absolutely. So tell me, *Alyx*—" he emphasized her name, "—what's wrong?"

Blowing out a breath, she dabbed at her eyes again. "The grand duke sent me a necklace with my family crest on it. He sent it via an old friend of his—I'm assuming that has some meaning, because you know, you don't ask your friends to look up pretenders to the family and deliver a royal crest on an exquisite piece of jewelry."

"No, that definitely has meaning." Victor checked the door lock, then walked across the room to run a washcloth under cold water.

"So that kind of has me nervous about actually meeting him tonight. Mr. Prentiss said that I was the spitting image of our great-grandmother. It's why the grand duke accepted me as a family member without meeting me." She glanced down at the necklace nestled in the black velvet box on the vanity of the dressing room they'd taken over.

Victor crossed back over to her and plucked the tissue from her hands and replaced it with the cold cloth. One hand on her shoulder, he guided her over to the settee and nodded to it. "Sit—put that over your eyes and let's see if we can get the swelling out."

"My dress," she protested. Yet another lesson he'd hammered home. When dressed for the evening, avoid sitting as much as possible to minimize the lines and wrinkles marring the outfit.

"We can take care of it. Sit." He glared at her until she did as he ordered and pressed the cold cloth to her overheated eyes. She wanted to weep with relief. He arranged a pillow so she put her head all the way back, then moved away. The water turned on again. "Continue."

"Why do you think there's more?" She didn't want to confess everything. Feeling a fool was one thing, admitting it something else. After all, she'd been born in the real world where there were real consequences for stupid actions.

"Because the grand duke's gesture of friendship and family is hardly worth crying yourself sick, no matter how shocking you may find it. Foster care taught you to retreat from close ties. I understand that and eventually, the grand duke will as well, but this is a reason to celebrate. Perhaps weep a little for the previously lost chances, but not sob as though your heart is broken."

She peeled the washcloth away from her eyes to peer at him. Victor returned with a fresh cold cloth and traded them out.

"So tell me. Why are you crying, Alyx?"

"I fell in love with him. He's wonderful. He's funny. He's kind. He's generous." The words spilled out in a rush and Victor wavered beyond the sheen of tears in her eyes. "I wasn't supposed to love him. I wasn't supposed to believe we could have something. It was all a masquerade, a charade to get his business deal." Saying it out loud made her feel worse than foolish. "He never lied to me, Victor. He never told me that he wanted a real affair. He was plain as day when he propositioned me and I understood the terms of the contract. I said no sex and then I had sex with him."

"I see." Victor cleared his throat.

She laughed, a wheezing noise, and lifted her hand, palm up. "A lot of sex, and I knew—from that very first kiss this was a bad idea—"

"Why?" he interrupted. "Why is it a bad idea?"

Pulling the cloth away, she stared at him. "He kissed me because you told him to."

"No." Victor shook his head slowly. "He kissed you because he wanted to. He protected you because he wanted to do that as well. I just gave him the excuse he was looking for."

"You can't know that." She frowned.

But what if he was right?

What if Daniel *had* wanted to kiss her? At Napa, they'd been alone in their bedroom and again in the limousine. They'd escaped into Big Bear alone.

Of course, by then they were already kissing and he was a man. Men had needs. God knew, she'd had them after those soul-scorching kisses. *Never mistake sex for love.* She had no idea which of her foster mothers told her that, but it was right about the time she'd reached sixteen and asked to go on the pill.

"Of course I can." Victor pushed the cloth back to her eyes. "Keep that on there. Your eyes are already looking better and we want all that puffiness gone."

"How can you *know*?"

"The same way I knew you really were a princess the first time I saw you. You possess an elegance and regal bearing that can't be taught. You needed some guidance and to believe in yourself and yes, the protocol lessons." He tweaked her pride, but the humor in his voice gentled any possible insult. "But all I did was polish what existed, brought out the diamond and made it shine."

"And you think Daniel wanted to kiss me?" She crossed mental fingers because she wanted so much for that to be true.

"Absolutely. From the first moment I met you, he hovered there, protective, but not intrusive. He took to touching you far easier than you did to being touched. He followed you with his eyes and enjoyed the kissing lessons. As, I am fairly certain, you did too. When you became lovers, I'm certain that was a choice on both your parts and it had nothing to do with the business deal. No matter what you might tell yourself, the two of you make a delicious couple and it was visible to all who watched you."

"Do you really think so?" She wasn't fishing for compliments or pushing further, she just couldn't escape the horrible certainty that she'd mucked everything up. Even worse than all of that was she'd taken their affair to heart and then fled rather than just confront him there. What if he'd told her she was right? That would have killed her.

"Well, if you want to finish what you started, Princess, take the negotiation to him publicly, then court him with a battle—if it is about you. He will fight for you. If it's just about the deal, he will avoid the scandal."

"What do you mean? Tell the world about the contract?" She wiped at her eyes.

"No, repudiate him. If you break up with him in public, make it a real fight—he'll either fight for you because *you* are who he wants or retreat to avoid that scandal that might hurt his business..."

That sounded really manipulative.

"I can't do that." She shook her head. She could never put Daniel on the spot like that. Not after everything else. Real affair or not, he'd been so damn kind to her. Maybe too kind, but she liked to think they were friends, and she didn't screw over her friends.

"Then you put on your prettiest face, you stand up there and meet your family and you re-member—Daniel Voldakov or not, you are the Grand Duchess Alyxandretta and you have a family and a position and friends all your own that have nothing to do with any deal." He squeezed her shoulder. "Remember, Princess, in fairy tales, the darkest moments come before the prince can rescue the princess."

More fairy tale shit?

The pain in her chest receded and she sat up slowly, giving him a wry smile. "But what if I turned my prince into a toad because I didn't think about what I was doing?"

"Then you must choose to risk your heart and decide what it is you want and then fight for it." He offered her a hand and she took it. "And that, my darling princess, is the end of our friendship time. We must usher you along if you are to be presentable this evening."

The smile that curved her lips this time felt genuine and lacked any waterworks. "Thank you, Victor."

He bowed, stern eyes relaxing with a hint of a twinkle. "It is my honor, Princess."

After that, he let the cosmetics and hair women back in. They made no exclamations over the wreck of her complexion or the muss of her hair, but bustled about getting her ready. She concentrated on breathing, staring at the necklace with the royal crest waiting for her to don it when the ladies were done.

She made acquaintances, but not friends. She committed to short-term projects and she always left before they could ask her to go. Rhonda called her adventurous—but it wasn't adventure, it was running away.

She never called her college roommate.

Or her foster mothers.

She'd focused on forgetting her foster siblings, particularly the younger ones—the hardest ones to say goodbye to.

If she didn't get close, she couldn't be hurt.

When Daniel took her to Sacramento, she'd stared at that strip mall where her house used to be and felt the devastating loss of that night all those years before. It was a lot like losing her parents all over again.

Only she didn't go home with a stranger.

She went home with Daniel. And no matter how much she rejected him, he didn't walk away from her. He gave her space, but he didn't abandon her. He fought with her, he challenged her and he backed her up against Victor.

And then he'd kissed her, held her, made her laugh until her sides hurt. He played with her and he talked to her.

He *played* with her.

Her stomach rippled.

"Victor?" She glanced up at the mirror, wildly aware of the women working on her face and her hair. He looked over at her, cell phone in his hand.

"Yes, Your Highness?"

"How do most fairy tales end?"

"It depends. Do you prefer the traditional tales or the Americanized version?"

She grinned. "I'm definitely an All-American kind of girl."

"Then happily. We have a plan?"

"Yes." She nodded slowly. "Yes, we do."

CHAPTER 21
DANIEL

aniel hated L.A. traffic. She stole his damn car. She'd stolen his car and left him. The resort offered him a driver, but he paid a fee to borrow their car and used the driving time to focus on his pitch to the grand duke. But frankly, he didn't give a damn about the consortium, the prince or his wardrobe. If his tux hadn't been laid out and ready for him when he arrived at home, yelling for Alyx, he would have just left it there. All the way home from Big Bear, her note haunted him.

What happened to the fun lover with her playful touches and erotic kisses? He'd left her sprawled and satisfied on the bed to shower, then walked out to find her gone and a note about a party with the grand duke and a stilted promise to meet him there. Why the hell hadn't she come in to tell me? They could have driven back together.

Unless the princess gig means a hell of a lot more to her than I do. And why shouldn't it? It's her family.

It's all she could possibly have wanted—a real family, real ties...

He scowled as the car in front of him lurched forward a few inches, only to slam on its brakes again.

He hit the button on the Bluetooth and told the phone to call Victor Russell. He'd already talked to Martin—his best friend was too busy chortling over the success of his insane plan to be of much use. He grimaced at the harsh thought—it was hardly Martin's fault that he'd let himself get caught up in the fantasy.

But what was more real?

The woman he found in her car or the princess who glided on his arm?

And does it really matter? You wanted her to be a princess. It just never occurred to you what would happen when that duckling turned into the swan, did it?

"Mr. Voldakov." Russell's stiff tone greeted him.

"You haven't by any chance seen my fiancée this afternoon, have you?" The fiancée who wasn't answering her cell phone, hadn't been at the house and had left him with a cryptic note and a case of self-examination the likes of which he hadn't experienced since the days he got bullied in high school.

"Why, yes, I just put her in a car on the way to the Beverly Hilton for the reception." The man's tone was cool. Too cool.

Eyes narrowing, Daniel glared at the traffic still insisting on inching its way forward. "And would you happen to know if she has her phone with her?"

"She did, but I'm afraid she forgot it in the rush to get ready. We had to pick out a new dress, shoes and accessories befitting her rank before her presentation to the grand duke."

Logical, reasoned responses to the invitation and all perfect in keeping with their original deal —but something was off.

"What aren't you telling me?"

"I am so pleased that you asked. The princess arrived for her personal shopping appointment very upset. It seems she's concerned that she broke her contract with you—heartsick, in fact."

His chest tightened. "How does she feel she broke it?"

"I would not be one to betray confidences, Mr. Voldakov. It is both a personal and moral affront."

Cagey bastard.

"I see." Daniel drummed his fingers. Every problem had a solution. The most difficult of bugs could be worked out if the programmer came at it from a different angle. "What was her state of mind when she left you?"

"Determined."

Determined to see their deal through? Determined to call him an ass? Determined to be the one woman in the world who could drive him mad with just a tilt of her head? Daniel swallowed the bitter bile of self-doubt and focused. "And would you have any sage wisdom you'd like to impart about this evening's events?"

"Possibly. But the question you should ask yourself is what are you willing to lose, Mr. Voldakov?"

Traffic opened up in front of him and he stared over the cars, barely moving his foot to the accelerator until a car honked noisily behind him. "What am I willing to lose?"

"Yes, sir. What are you willing to lose?"

"I'm not willing to lose her." No hesitation. No doubt.

To hell with the European deal, to hell with the consortium and thrice be damned to the royal clutch that held the contract strings. Spherecast was a phenomenal success without the damn EU. He had the keys to a Japanese contract and he'd get his foothold in Europe the another way—with hard work and sweat.

Hell, the company could go belly up and he'd build another, but what was the point without her?

He'd been an idiot to think it was all about business. He'd told that lie to everyone who mattered. Most of all, he'd said it to her.

"Then tell the princess the truth." It was as though he'd heard every word played out in Daniel's mental argument.

"That's your advice?"

"It is." The cool and detached words reflected the man himself. "Tell her it's not about the fantasy. Tell her about your reality and her place in it."

Could he do that? Could he walk in there and put his heart all on the line? What if, by some ironic accident of fate, he'd pushed her to become the very type of woman he didn't want? But the moment the thought tried to take root in his mind, he pictured her sitting cross-legged and naked in the middle of the bed, laughing at something the cat did on the British science fiction show.

That was the woman he'd fallen in love with —barren of any artifice, gem or cosmetic. The pure, open, cheerful woman with the easy smile and the quick wit.

The woman who shut down when her hopes were ripped away. The woman who fought to survive and pursued her dreams.

She was part of the woman he loved too.

"Mr. Voldakov?" Russell's voice punched through his reverie and thankfully, traffic achieved thirty miles an hour.

"Russell. Did I break something in her?"

"Bent, perhaps, but not broken. Be honest. Tell her the truth. You have to be willing to take on the dragon with no certainty of success if you want to get your princess back."

Take on the dragon.

"Thanks, Russell."

"You're welcome, Mr. Voldakov."

He hit the button on the steering wheel to end the call. He'd walk through fire for Alyx, so swallowing his pride shouldn't be that much more difficult.

An hour later, he tossed his keys to the valet and circled his car to walk into the hotel. He didn't slow his stride. It was after seven and while he'd hoped to find her in the lobby waiting for him, he strode toward the elevators and took them to the ballroom level. Security waited for him just outside the doors. He passed them his ID and waited impatiently for his name to be checked off the list.

Tell her the truth. Russell's words rang in his ears. Martin would kill him. But he already wanted to shred that contract and more—he wanted to shed the whole charade. He wanted the former waitress and aspiring actress to go out with him for ice-cream sundaes, watch midnight movies and help him design that identify-a-shoe app.

He wanted *her.*

At the entrance to the ballroom, he paused and let his eyes adjust. Skimming the crowd, he had no trouble finding her. She stood off to the side, arms wrapped around a tall European.

Quiet fury seethed up.

Tell her the truth.

He would tell her the truth—right after he told that fucking poacher to get his hands off her.

He barely saw the rest of the room as he strode over. He took the man by the arm and pulled him off of Alyx, the fingers of his left hand curling into a fist. Then he slammed it into the man's chiseled, elegant jaw.

"Daniel!" Alyx let out a little cry, but he pinned the fallen fellow. Somewhere in the back of his brain, he recognized his face and his features. But in this moment, he couldn't quite see past the haze of anger to acknowledge that recognition.

"She's taken. Learn to keep your hands to yourself." He turned to catch Alyx's arm and spun her toward the door, marching her out of the room with as much dignity as he could muster while her attention focused behind them.

Martin's stunned face among the crowd of gawkers barely penetrated his periphery. The music hiccupped as everyone stared, but someone must have said something, because it began again.

Outside the ballroom, Daniel steered Alyx away from the security and other onlookers until he crowded her into a private nook. Once there, he let out a breath and stared at her. She was dressed in the most basic black, a pair of diamond studs glittered in her ears and the only other jewelry the royal crest necklace the grand duke sent her. A pair of artfully placed clips in her hair gave the illusion of a tiara and the overall effect was absolutely stunning.

"You're beautiful." That wasn't exactly how he planned to start the conversation, but it definitely bore repeating. "Absolutely beautiful."

She jerked her arm out of his grasp.

"Why on earth did you hit him?" She stared at him with traces of sadness that echoed his own upset in her wide eyes.

"Because he was touching you. And I don't care who he is, you're not available."

"Oh really?" Her chin came up and she put a hand on her hip. "I'm not?"

"No." He slid an arm around her and pulled her close. "You're not." He slanted his mouth over hers and poured all of his frustration and want into that kiss. She caught hold of his jacket, hanging on to him. At first he thought she'd push him away, but she tugged him closer and for the first time since walking out of the shower to the empty cabin, the shackles on his heart snapped.

"You're taken, Miss Dagmar," he murmured against her lips. "One hundred and ten percent."

She sighed beneath his kiss and bit down on his lip when he would have taken it further. He blinked at the sharp nip of pain and lifted his head to look at her. "I know what our contract said—"

"To hell with our contract." He interrupted her. "In fact, we can burn it together when we get home. I don't care about what you agreed to or what I offered—I want to negotiate new terms."

She blinked slowly. "Dare I ask what those terms might be?"

"Well, the first is that you agree to go out with me on a real date—one where we don't worry about photo opportunities or elegance. Just fun."

"I see." The hesitation in her face robbed him of breath.

Rushing on, he held her hands up between them. "The second part is you let me put a real ring on this finger. Not for show, not for a deal and not for any other reason than that I asked you to marry me."

Her pupils dilated and he heard the quick catch in her breath.

"Daniel, we—we barely know each other."

"You like ice cream in the middle of the night. You adore British science fiction shows. You refuse to put value on things because you're always worried they're going to be taken away. You love having a home, but you aren't sure you actually belong in one. You're a princess who doesn't believe she is one. You're a woman with a big heart and a love for make-believe."

"I know you too. You're a dreamer and fixer." Her lower lip trembled, but her voice was steady. "You like to build things and solve puzzles and you're way too generous for your own good, but sometimes you miss the really big things right in front of you. I know because—because I miss them too."

Tell her the truth.

He took a deep breath and flung it out there, facing off with the dragon with no real assurance that he would be successful.

He dropped to one knee.

"I don't need a business deal to be happy or to write anything more than basic code. You're the woman I love, Alyx, and I don't care what title you want to put on that as long as it means you're with me for the rest of my life."

She swallowed and tears glossed over her eyes. One tremulous drop slid down her cheek and she held his heart in her keeping. He gazed up at her and tried to infuse everything he was feeling into his gaze. *Believe me.*

"If it has any bearing on your decision at all, cousin, I approve." A deep, masculine voice with a European accent interrupted. Daniel ignored it, staring up at her. The pressure on his chest eased when she didn't look away either.

"Yes." One word. Just one. And he stood and lifted her into his arms, kissing her. He heard her laughter, tasted her tears and did his absolute best not to whoop. But the wild applause breaking out around them forced him to lift his head. Most of the ballroom had followed them out to the secluded corner, including the man nursing a faintly reddening bruise.

"Well done, Mr. Voldakov. Well done." The man, it seemed, was also leading the applause. He stepped toward them and held out his hand. "Armand Dagmar."

Well, that explained Martin's apoplectic expression and the niggle of recognition. He'd slugged the grand duke.

"Call me Daniel, Your Highness." He accepted the man's firm handshake.

"It would be my pleasure." The grand duke glanced over his shoulder and security moved in to usher the crowd back to the ballroom, leaving them in relative privacy. "I would be honored if you would call me Armand."

Alyx held tightly to Daniel's arm and he leaned over to brush a kiss to her forehead. "I'm going to guess you two have already introduced yourselves."

"Um, yeah." It was her turn to laugh. "Armand was just apologizing to me that the family never came for me. They'd never known my father married, much less had a child."

The grand duke inclined his head, genuine sorrow turning his mouth down. "Precisely. Your grandfather and mine were brothers, but they quarreled over a woman, of all things. My grandmother, as it happens. Your grandfather moved to the States in a fit of pique. We knew he'd married and had a son, but he moved frequently and refused to call the family. My grandfather was equally stubborn and wouldn't pursue the matter. A few years ago, when my grandfather passed, my father tried to locate your family, only to learn both were deceased." Armand sighed. "Had we known you existed, we would have taken every measure to bring you back to our family. If you believe nothing else, please believe that."

He held out his hand and Alyx took it, her smile sad, but without any regret. "I do, and thank you. As grateful as I am for the idea, I have to say I'm glad you didn't."

Daniel raised his eyebrows and swung a look down at his fiancée—fiancée sounded almost as good as wife. "Sweetheart..."

"No." She shook her head and looked between them. "Seriously, if I had been rescued and taken back to Europe, I wouldn't have met you, Daniel. I wouldn't have been in my car when you knocked on the window and... No...I wouldn't trade that for anything."

Armand chuckled softly and, with a half-wary glance at Daniel, leaned in to kiss her cheek.

"You have my heartiest congratulations, cousin. A determined man, indeed, you've found. I have a feeling he will do well in our family. Contracts notwithstanding."

"About the hit earlier..." Daniel began.

Armand waved away his apology and if he had any problem with the other bit of information, he didn't share it. "What are a few bruises among family? Trust me, my brothers have hit me harder—and with less cause. Although I'm afraid your story will make quite the splash tomorrow." He glanced over his shoulder at the press being wrangled back. Daniel didn't care. They could print anything they wanted. He had Alyx.

The three fell silent and Armand squeezed her hand. "For now, I will leave the two of you to your private celebration. Feel free to take the suite upstairs, I will let security know you may have it." He straightened his tie. "It's time for me to shock the locals and see if any of the local celebutantes have shown up."

With a rakish wink, he spun on a heel and marched away.

"He's not bad for a prince."

"No," Alyx agreed and slipped her arms around him. "But I prefer my regular Americans with their software billions to any old-fashioned European playboys."

"Good to know." He stared down at her. "Why did you leave?"

"Because I'm an idiot?" She shook her head slowly. "Martin called and said the grand duke was here and he was ecstatic that their attorneys were beginning the slow dance to hire Spherecast and he was overwhelming in his compliments about the success of your 'plan.'"

He'd thought as much, but hearing the forlorn note in her voice, he wished they could go back to that moment the phone rang. He would have smashed it for her. "Why didn't you tell me?"

"Because we had a deal. You wanted a princess to get a business contract." She sighed, a note of impatience in her voice. "Of course, I overreacted and I was going to make it up to you by having the deal all in place and then offering to stay on, permanently. You know to keep it going. But not as a princess—as just me. This is the role of a lifetime, one I wanted for me. Not just to play. Everything we did—it was all working to that goal."

"Everything?" He lifted his brows.

"Well, almost everything. I didn't really care about your contract in Napa Valley."

"Glad to hear it. I don't think I've worried about it in weeks." He laughed, pulling her close and resting his chin against her hair. Music drifted out of the ballroom and the security guards drew back to a nice distance, keeping away the onlookers, but letting them have their privacy.

"Why didn't you say something?"

"Pride? Stubbornness? Who knows? I'm stupid?" He grinned. "I'm just glad I didn't wait too long."

"Me too." She squeezed him. "Although, I had a plan."

"You did?"

"Hmm-hmm. Victor told me that if I wanted my happily ever after, I had to keep kissing my toad—"

"Toad?" He interrupted, not sure he liked where this was going.

"It's just a figure of speech."

"Uh-huh. Go on." He swayed with her, enjoying the weight of her against his body, her lean softness to his harder height.

"Anyway, he reminded me that American fairy tales have happily ever afters. So I was going to surrender my 'duchy' before they could give it to me and ask you for a job at your software company."

He blinked. "How is that a plan?"

"I would have made sure you put a 'sexual harassment required' clause in my contract." The wry, saucy response tickled him and he leaned back.

"I'll sexually harass you anytime you want."

"Excellent." She grinned. "Does that go both ways?"

"Baby, you have to promise to sexually harass me—just do it when you're naked." He waggled his eyebrows.

"Why naked?"

"Why not?"

They laughed.

Inside the ballroom, the music faded and a round of applause drew their attention. Arm in arm, they drifted toward the door. Daniel didn't really care what was happening inside, but he would never ask her to give up her newfound family.

Royal or not.

The grand duke stood in the center of the room, a microphone in hand. "Good evening all and thank you for attending this event with us tonight. Most of you here are dear friends or steady colleagues. You have been with our family for years, so you are the first that I wanted to introduce to our latest members—one who has deserved to be here from the moment of her birth, and the other, the very fortunate man who won her heart. Please help me to welcome my cousin, the Grand Duchess Alyxandretta, princess royal, and her future husband—he with a mean left hook—Daniel Voldakov."

The spotlight swung across the room and illuminated them in the doorway. The applause rippled across the room. Alyx leaned close to him and murmured, "You realize there's no getting out of this now?"

"I wouldn't want it any other way." He caught her hand and guided her out onto the dance floor among the applause. When the waltz came on, he pulled her into his arms and pressed his lips to her ear. "My princess."

"And they lived happily...ever...after."

"Damn straight."

CHAPTER 22
ALYX

S ix months later...

ALYX STARED at the dress in the mirror. The white chiffon spilled down to the floor, while the lace bodice hugged her chest while diamonds and flowers decorated her hair. She'd refused the offer of a tiara, but when Armand requested the right to walk her down the aisle, she didn't turn him down.

They'd come a long way in the six months since they'd met—vacationing in Belgium with him and his siblings, as well as meeting up in New York twice, and once more in Los Angeles during the engagement party. The only true argument erupted when it came to the wedding venue. Armand wanted to host her wedding at the family estate in Norway. But she had no ties to that place, not yet. Daniel preferred Los Angeles, but was pretty much willing for anything—except the drive-through Elvis chapel she'd suggested.

They'd compromised and chosen a sleepy little church in Woodland. Her parents had been married there. Both families agreed and the city of Sacramento's tourism board threw in help with security as royal watchers from around the world flocked to see their simple wedding. When a certain British prince appeared on the guest list, they'd had to double their security conditions.

"You look radiant," Rhonda complimented and kissed her cheek. She'd chosen Rhonda for her maid of honor and Lucy for her bridesmaid. Daniel's secretary tried to refuse, but she insisted and Daniel swore he'd call her morning, noon and night until she agreed.

Standing best man for Daniel was Martin.

As part of their wedding present, he'd hosted a beachside bonfire, burning their contract while they toasted marshmallows. Even Daniel's mother was in the crowd, along with Grace Burrows from the social services office. The chapel could only hold about a hundred and fifty guests, so the rest of their wedding guests waited for them at the ballroom of the Grand Hotel where they would celebrate the reception.

Armand arrived with both of his brothers—Sebastian and George. George was by far her favorite, just two years her junior and with a deep interest in film. They'd hit it off during the first vacation and she'd promised him a tour of Hollywood after the honeymoon...

The top-secret honeymoon that only Victor knew the destination of, because he'd taken care of getting her clothes ready.

Personally, she didn't care where they were going. With the craziness of the wedding plans, the Takahashi contract and the recently announced European deals, she and Daniel hadn't had five minutes alone together. Armand insisted they spend the night before the wedding apart and he'd hosted her at his recently acquired Petersburg Tower along with the rest of the family, including two dowager aunts, a haphazard collection of cousins and his brothers.

He'd given her a ring for Daniel—she could give it to him after the ceremony. Like her necklace, it carried the family crest and declared him an official member of the Andraste royal family. From blue-collar billionaire to member of the pedigree'd elite, who would have imagined that a random dinner appointment with his attorney would have sat them in her station and led to this day?

"Are you ready, beautiful cousin?" Armand stood in the doorway. She could hear the first stirrings of the music as Rhonda and Lucy preceded her up the aisle.

She exhaled and he held out his arm. So much pomp and circumstance, but none of it mattered. Armand guided her down the hallway and the double doors to the chapel opened. Inside the guests stood and a single photographer, one approved by the family and vetted by Daniel, took her picture. The first bars of the wedding march echoed through the chapel, but Alyx heard none of it.

Standing at the end of that long walk was the sun god who woke her from a long and lonely sleep. She forced Armand to pick up the pace.

She couldn't wait for their happily ever after.

EPILOGUE

ALYX

Andraste Grand Duke Armand walked his recently discovered cousin, the Grand Duchess Alyxandretta, down the aisle in Sacramento today. Royal watchers from around the world flooded the city and jammed up YouTube with impromptu video coverage after the family declined to air the wedding on national television. While not invited to the wedding itself, the First Lady and the vice president were invited to the reception along with some two thousand other dignitaries.

The happy couple includes groom Daniel Voldakov, a self-made billionaire and sole owner of Spherecast Technologies. The software giant employs nearly seven hundred people in the Los Angeles area. The fairy tale love story for Grand Duchess will be the subject of a cable movie, The Billionaire and his Pauper Princess. It's rumored that the grand duchess herself will have a role in the film.

In the meanwhile, royal hopefuls have their

eye on the playboy Grand Duke Armand. He broke up with his on-again-off-again girlfriend, model Nikole duMonde, last month in Monte Carlo. We have to wonder if his cousin's nuptials gave the model ideas and the confirmed bachelor sought to curb her chances at catching the bouquet.

So, which lucky lady will catch his eye next? We can only standby for further developments.

Back to you, Bob.

"What lucky lady will catch his eye next?" Alyx laughed as she clicked off the entertainment report. "After all the cameras outside the hotel, I think *that* lucky lady would have to want to live under a microscope to set her sights on him."

"Hmm, possibly." They were sprawled in the room of their borrowed Napa estate. Daniel, with Armand and Victor's help, led the paparazzi on a merry chase. The press thought they were flying out, but instead, they'd driven off in Alyx's old car of all things.

While everyone searched for a limousine, they'd made their escape in the ten-year-old Volvo.

Daniel traced a finger down her bare leg. "Any regrets?"

She glanced at him, then the crest ring he'd slid on next to his wedding ring. "None. You?"

"Yes." He nodded solemnly.

Worry bloomed in her chest. He'd insisted on a fast wedding, splitting the difference with her family for six months, rather than their traditional one-year engagement.

She'd been tempted to toss the whole lot, but after seeing how much Armand enjoyed giving her away, and the faces of those friends that were near and dear to them, she'd been satisfied with the choice. "What's wrong?"

"You're still sitting at the end of the bed, when I have all this wonderful room up here."

"Mean," Alyx accused, laughter writhing through the anxiety. She grabbed a pillow and pounced forward, swinging.

"Foul!" He roared playfully and swatted her with a pillow of his own. They beat on each other until his pillow exploded and he cried mercy. But her moment of triumph was short-lived as he swept her down onto the bed and pinned her in a scorching kiss.

Breathlessly she stared up at him and then pinched his shoulder.

"Ow." He grinned. "What did I do?"

"Everything. I just have to keep reminding myself that you're real."

"Oh, I'm definitely real." He kissed her again as if to prove his point. "And if you keep pinching me, I won't give you your wedding present."

"You got me a present?"

"Hmm-hmm." He grinned and rolled over to open the bedside drawer. She didn't know when he'd secreted the present in, but she sat up to accept the flat package wrapped in red and gold foil. No name tag or bow offset the plain elegance of the wrap.

"What is it?"

"Open it." He laughed, resting a hand on her thigh.

She shook it once. "I don't hear keys."

"Nope. It's not a new car, but you are getting one."

"I like my Volvo." She stuck her tongue out at him.

"Me too. It will make a lovely cube of metal for some modern art collection." He squeezed her leg. "Go on, open it."

"Hmm." She put the foil-wrapped box to her forehead. "The Great Karnac sees all and knows all—" She squinted at him. "It's a ticket for endless wonder."

"Open it," he repeated patiently, his eyes twinkling. "Silly wife."

Her heart melted. "Say it again."

His eyebrows lifted. "What, open it?"

"No. The other part."

"Silly wife?" He grinned. "I like the sound of that. Wife."

"Me too." And the tears gathered in her eyes again. He didn't ask, just sat up and tugged her into his arms, holding her tight. It was so hard to get used to—this sense of permanence in her life of transience.

But Daniel loved her. Daniel married her.

He may have helped her rediscover her roots, but he'd become her family.

He pressed a kiss to her forehead. "Open the box."

Sniffling, she swiped at her tears and slit the

paper up the seam with her nail. The plain white box inside betrayed nothing of its contents. Daniel crumpled the paper and tossed it toward the wastebasket. She slit the tape on the edges of the box and pulled open the lid.

"Oh my God." The earlier tears surged with a vengeance and the photograph in the simple black frame swam in front of her.

"It's the best I could do."

"Daniel?" She looked up at him. "It's my mom and dad."

"I know, baby. You're there too. See?" He pointed to her mom's belly and she had to blink furiously to see past the tears. Her parents were sitting outside, under a very familiar tree. Her dad's arms were around her mom and they were laughing at the camera. Her mother's swollen belly revealed her pregnancy.

"How?" He'd found a photo. She saw herself in her father, the shape of her ears, the jut of her chin. She looked just like her father. And like Armand—they had the same eyes.

"We found a woman named Kelly Kensington. She was your mom's best friend and the maid of honor at her wedding—"

"The chapel." She looked up. "When you told me about it."

"Yep. It occurred to my P.I. that their marriage had to be recorded somewhere and there was at least a small chance that so would their witnesses. After that, it was just a matter of finding them. Ms. Kensington had this in her photo album and a couple more from when you were a baby. They're all at home waiting for you. But this one—this one I wanted you to have now."

"I love you." She wrapped her arms around him and he pulled her close.

"I love you."

He gave her everything.

He was her forever family.

AFTERWORD

It's always a pleasure to share an old favorite with new people. If you enjoyed this, keep an eye out for more old favorites to return after I they get re-edited and updated. Also, if you want to check out more of my stuff, I can't wait to see what you think!

xoxo
Heather

Website:
heatherlong.net
Reader group:
facebook.com/groups/heatherspack
Spoiler group:
facebook.com/groups/teammadatheather

About Heather Long

I *love* books. Not just a little bit, but a lot. Books were my best friends when I was growing up. Books didn't care if I was new to a town or to a class. They were always there, my trustiest of companions. Until they turned on me and said I had to write them.

I can tell you that my own personal happily ever after included writing books. I've always said that an HEA is a work in progress. It's true in my marriage, my friendships, and in my career. I am constantly nurturing my muse as we dive into new tales, new tropes, new characters and more.

After seventeen years in Texas, we relocated to the Pacific Northwest in search of seasons, new experiences, and new geography. I can't wait to discover what life (and my muse) have in store for me.

Maybe writing was always my destiny and romance my fate. After all, my grandmother wasn't a fan of picture books and used to read me her Harlequin Romance novels.

Follow Heather & Sign up for her newsletter:
www.heatherlong.net
TikTok

Also by Heather Long

82nd Street Vandals

Savage Vandal

Vicious Rebel

Ruthless Traitor

Dirty Devil

Shamelessly Loyal (Novella)

Brutal Fighter

Dangerous Renegade

Merciless Spy

Reckless Thief

Fierce Dancer

Dirty Dancer

Bay Ridge Royals

Shamelessly Loyal (Novella)

Battle Lines

Deceptive Truce

Wicked Surrender

Violent Chaos

Desperate Victory

BLOOD Brothers

Burn

Lure

Blue Ivy Prep

Problem Child

Mad Boys

Party Crashers

Money Shot

Bravo Team Wolf

When Danger Bites

Bitten Under Fire

Cardinal Sins

Kill Song

First Chorus

High Note

Last Word

Chance Monroe

Earth Witches Aren't Easy

Plan Witch from Out of Town

Bad Witch Rising

Fevered Hearts

Marshal of Hel Dorado

Brave are the Lonely

Micah & Mrs. Miller

A Fistful of Dreams

Raising Kane

Wanted: Fevered or Alive

Wild and Fevered

The Quick & The Fevered

A Man Called Wyatt

Heart of the Nebula

Queenmaker

Deal Breaker

Throne Taker

Lone Star Leathernecks

Semper Fi Cowboy

As You Were, Cowboy

Shackled Souls

Succubus Chained

Succubus Unchained

Succubus Blessed

Shackled Souls (Omnibus)

STANDALONES

Kiss of Fate (w/Blake Blessing)

Taste of Karma (w/Blake Blessing)

I'll Be Home... (w/Tate James)

Overexposed (w/Tate James)

Switchboard Duet

Talk to Me

Don't Let Go

Untouchable

Rules and Roses

Changes and Chocolates

Keys and Kisses

Whispers and Wishes

Hangovers and Holidays

Brazen and Breathless

Trials and Tiaras

Graduation and Gifts

Defiance and Dedication

Songs and Sweethearts

Legacy and Lovers

Farewells and Forever

Hellos and Happily Ever Afters

Wolves of Willow Bend

Wolf at Law

Wolf Bite

Caged Wolf

Wolf Claim

Wolf Next Door

Rogue Wolf

Bayou Wolf

Untamed Wolf

Wolf with Benefits

River Wolf

Single Wicked Wolf

Desert Wolf

Snow Wolf

Wolf on Board

Holly Jolly Wolf

Shadow Wolf

His Moonstruck Wolf

Thunder Wolf

Ghost Wolf

Outlaw Wolves

Wolf Unleashed